As she watched Rowan, Lady Maisie saw the child start upright in her seat, eyes staring, almost in fact as though she had seen a ghost. Automatically, Lady Maisie checked herself for visibility. It was many years since she'd been powerful enough to come into plain sight, and she was certain that she remained unseen. The child must have been frightened by something else. The ghost followed Rowan's gaze and saw that the person at whom she was staring with such horror was a shabby, bearded young man wearing a foppish furred hat with a long peak drawn over his face. What was so alarming about him? He was slumped in the back row, rather out of place amongst the mainly elderly women, but scarcely sinister. Curious, the ghost allowed herself to drift down in his direction – and no sooner was she within the young man's orbit than she found her nose twitching and her ears buzzing.

There was mischief in the air . . .

www.kidsatrandomhouse.co.uk

Also by Helen Dunwoodie:

Published by Corgi Yearling Books:

GHOST ON THE LOOSE

Published by Corgi Books:

SOLO ACT

HELEN DUNWOODIE

Ghost
to the
Rescue!

CORGI YEARLING BOOKS

GHOST TO THE RESCUE
A CORGI YEARLING BOOK : 0 440 864216

First publication in Great Britain

PRINTING HISTORY
Corgi Yearling edition published 2001

3 5 7 9 10 8 6 4 2

Set in 12.5/15.5pt Century Schoolbook
by Phoenix Typesetting, Ilkley, West Yorkshire

Corgi Yearling Books are published by Random House Children's Books,
61–63 Uxbridge Road, London W5 5SA,
a division of The Random House Group Ltd,
in Australia by Random House Australia (Pty) Ltd,
20 Alfred Street, Milsons Point, Sydney, NSW 2061, Australia,
in New Zealand by Random House New Zealand Ltd,
18 Poland Road, Glenfield, Auckland 10, New Zealand
and in South Africa by Random House (Pty) Ltd,
Endulini, 5a Jubilee Road, Parktown 2193, South Africa.

Made and printed in Great Britain by
Cox & Wyman Ltd, Reading, Berkshire

With thanks to the Scottish Arts Council
for their generous support
And with love to disco lions, operatic tigers
and Buffy fans everywhere

ONE

Lady Maisie McNeil was comfortably asleep in a hammock fashioned from a magnetic charge and then knotted firmly to a ley line. This was a usual method of slumber for a ghost, so while she drowsed, invisibly suspended above the shores of Loch Rannoch, she was lost in dreams of her glorious past.

However, as she slept, the ley line tightened, a ripple ran through it and the air around Lady Maisie sizzled. Slowly, unconsciously, the ghost began to drift eastwards, drawn towards her country's capital by a pulse of energy which she could not resist.

Lady Maisie was needed in Edinburgh.
When she awoke, she would discover why.

Rowan ran her fingers over a small package.
The rough brown paper and coarse string
were slightly greasy and smelt mysteriously
of fish. She lifted it to her nose, sniffed
cautiously, and then bravely sniffed again.
She'd been on the right track with fish. The
little parcel smelt as though it had been
knocking about for weeks in Alice's backpack,
which had then been either tossed casually on
the deck of a trawler or lugged up a salmon
river. Because it *had* to be a present from
Alice. Rowan peered yet again at the smudged
postmark, the torn stamps, and her own name
and address, scrawled in capitals with a black
pen.

Or rather, her name, and that of her sister,
Bryony. Rowan tugged gently at the string,
but the knots held firm. It would be impossible to open the package and close it up again
without Bryony suspecting mischief. Rowan
almost moaned in frustration. She'd just have
to wait until the afternoon and Bryony's
return. The elder girl had already left as she
had a long bus ride to her old school, whilst

Rowan, who had changed schools when they had all moved in with Robert, Mum's boyfriend, only had a short walk.

Rowan sighed and gave the package a final squeeze. Of course, she told herself firmly, it might be something really boring and educational. An Afghanistan butter-press. A Siberian fossil. But she didn't really think so. Alice, Robert's ex-wife, last seen heading for Inner Mongolia and points north, had not struck Rowan as the sort of person who would send boring presents.

But Mongolia? Something didn't fit. Rowan looked again at the stamps. American! And didn't the postmark start with the letters AL? Could Alice have landed up in Alaska? But for Alice, who shone in Rowan's memory from their one meeting as an intrepid warrior-queen, anything was possible. She could easily have trekked by yak or pony all the way to Siberia and then travelled onwards to Alaska by fishing boat – which would account for the smell of the intriguing parcel.

Completely absorbed in the mystery, Rowan was startled to hear footsteps scurrying down the hall towards the kitchen. Not the softy steady pad of Alice's tall leather boots but the dainty steps of someone wearing high-heeled slippers. Automatically, Rowan shoved the package into her schoolbag and fixed a bright, bland smile onto her face as Mum entered the room. It was not a good idea to mention Alice too often in Petronella's presence.

'Was that the post I heard, darling?' Despite being eight months pregnant, Petronella was as light on her feet as ever. She glided across the kitchen, the ruffles on her long, silky dressing-gown rippling out behind her like a train of little fishes.

'Just some stuff for Robert,' said Rowan, pushing a big stack of envelopes across the table. Robert, a well-known writer, received loads of mail, even fan-letters, although Rowan couldn't understand how anyone could actually read his slushy, romantic novels, far less write to thank him. But they did.

'Your warm-hearted book brightened a cold winter's day for me. Keep up the good work.' or *'Every one of your stories transports me to wonderful realms of fantasy. How can I thank you for the hours of joy which you have given me?'* Actually, many of the hours of joy

were due to Robert's mother, who had begun the Marjorie Gloaming historical novel series, but Robert, who had taken on the name after her death, was perfectly happy to take all the credit as well.

'More fan-letters, by the looks of them. I don't know why they bother.'

'But Robert's work brings pleasure to thousands!' cried Petronella, tossing her blond head. 'Think of all these weary housewives and tired businesswomen, sinking down gratefully at the end of the day, only too happy to forget themselves in *A Scots Bluebell*.'

'Oh yeah,' muttered Rowan, as she zipped up her bag and reached for her scarf and blazer. She knew perfectly well that Mum shared her own opinion of Robert's work, but was too loyal to say so.

'You are coming to the reading on Friday, aren't you?' Petronella paused in the act of making herself a mug of camomile tea.

'Suppose so,' said Rowan reluctantly.

'Now, you know it would mean a lot to Robert to have us all there. Bryony's coming so it would be so sweet if you came too. Like a real family.'

Robert was reading extracts from his

latest novel *The Lassie wi' the White Rose* at a local bookstore.

'All right,' said Rowan ungraciously. She might be doing her best to like Robert, but he was never going to be her real father. Rowan couldn't actually remember *him*, as he had shaken himself free from family responsibilities when she was a baby, but she was sure he wasn't a twit like Robert.

'He did alter the whole plot just to please you. You were the one who said that the heroine should be less wimpish to appeal to a modern audience.'

'But he was using a true story. The *real* Lady Maisie wasn't a wimp so it wasn't right to make her out to be a complete fool.'

'And Robert admitted you were right! So going to the reading is the very least you can do.'

'I said I'd go, didn't I?' Rowan heaved her bag onto her shoulder and tramped crossly towards the back door, but before she could reach it, she was halted by a small yelp from Petronella.

'They've come at last! And just in time!' She was clutching a long brown envelope which she had extracted from the fan-mail.

'What's come?'

Petronella didn't answer. She scuttled out into the hall, calling, 'Robert, darling, come here this minute and open this envelope! I think it must be you-know-what!'

Honestly, Mum behaved as though Rowan were a baby rather than almost a teenager. The thrilling letter was obviously something she wasn't supposed to know about. All right then, let Mum keep her daft secrets. She didn't care. Rowan took another step towards the door but Robert, too excited to share Petronella's qualms, burst into the kitchen.

'Is it? Is it?' cried Petronella.

Robert tore open the envelope and scanned the enclosed document. 'At last!' he cried, and Petronella flung herself dramatically into his arms.

Rowan regarded the scene with disgust. Robert was wearing one of his beautifully cut dark suits and with Mum being in her frilly dressing-gown they looked like an old-fashioned painting of a wife either welcoming her husband back from battle or begging him not to go.

Except, of course, that Mum and Robert weren't married.

'What is it?' Rowan suddenly felt very alarmed. 'What's happened?'

Robert and Petronella gave separate, guilty little jumps and stared at Rowan.

'Oh nothing, darling, just some boring old business letters.' Mum's pretty face, already flushed with happiness, turned even pinker.

'No, Petronella sweetheart, there's no point in keeping it a secret, the girls will know soon enough.' Robert looked both noble and commanding, his favourite expression, as he turned towards Rowan. 'These are the papers which declare my divorce from Alice to be final.'

'So we can get married at last!' cried Petronella, clasping her little white hands to her pin-tucked bodice.

'Married?' Rowan felt as though she'd been squeezed suddenly, and very hard, by some huge, invisible animal.

'Yes, we were just waiting for the papers. Everything's been held up by Alice being constantly out of touch on these wanderings of hers.'

'And now we can get married before the baby comes!' Petronella was almost skipping with delight. 'Everything signed and sealed!'

'But darling, won't it be too much for you – all the arrangements—?'

'Now don't be a silly old bear! I've got ages to go, and it only takes fifteen days for a marriage licence to come through. And it's not as though we were going to have a big affair, just something dignified and romantic.'

How could getting married when eight months pregnant possibly be dignified? thought Rowan.

'Isn't it exciting? You and Bryony can be bridesmaids!'

Bridesmaids! A cold shudder ran through Rowan's entire body.

'I thought you said it was going to be a small wedding?' said Robert, the first tiny touch of fear showing in his fine brown eyes.

Petronella ran one finger winsomely down his lapel. 'Not just small, absolutely *tiny*. I promise. And the girls don't have to be *bridesmaids* exactly. Attendants. Ladies-in-waiting.' Petronella could never quite forget her actress past in which she had several times swept onstage followed by a whole retinue of pages, courtiers and indeed, ladies-in-waiting.

Robert's expression softened. 'I'm sure

that whatever you decide will be just wonderful.'

Rowan reached for the back door and very quietly unlocked it – but not quietly enough. As the bolt clicked back, Petronella was jolted out of her bridal dream. 'Rowan, you're not going to be late for school, are you? Silly me, it's all my fault for keeping you back.'

'I'll be in time.'

'And you *are* pleased, aren't you, darling?'

'Just over the moon,' said Rowan, and then managed, finally, to duck out of the door before Mum could advance upon her for a farewell kiss. If there was one thing which Rowan disliked, it was having to bend over or around Robert's unborn child. How could Mum, who had always been so proud of her petite figure, bear being pregnant, especially when she already had two perfectly good children?

And now she was not only having Robert's baby, but also marrying him. Rowan supposed that she'd known all along that they would get married once Robert was divorced, but this had seemed so far away that she'd managed to ignore it. And why should she worry about it anyway? Mum and Robert actually being married wasn't to going to make any real difference to her life. It was just so, well, *final*.

Rowan stopped on the path and looked around the little garden. There were the beds of roses, still in flower, which old Mrs Monteith had planted, the grass plot, the mossy stone shepherdess. From now on, this really would be her home.

There was a rustle from under the hedge and Rowan turned to see her friend Atholl, who had been waiting for the slam of the back door, come trotting out to greet her. Atholl was a small, white Scottie dog, the property of their elderly next-door neighbour, Miss McFadzean. Rowan often took him out for a long walk at the weekends to make up for the quiet strolls he normally took with his mistress. Now she bent down and held his front paws as he tried to scrabble lovingly against her tights.

'Darling Atholl, who's furry? Who's handsome? It's all right for you, you haven't got to get all dolled-up to be a bridesmaid. You haven't got to have Robert for your stepfather.'

The little animal rubbed his white head against her tartan school skirt.

'Yes, I know, I wish we could go for a walk as well, but I've got to go to school. Anyway, look at those clouds, it's probably going to pour any minute, it wouldn't be any fun.' And giving him a final pat, Rowan let herself out into the lane which ran behind the back gardens of Dryburgh Place, whilst Atholl pressed his nose desolately against the bars of the gate.

Rowan sighed as she scuffed her way through the leaves which had drifted down from behind the high stone walls. She supposed that things had to change. Mum actually marrying that idiot Robert. And having a baby. And when that baby came, things would change more than ever. She wished she was old enough to leave home. She wouldn't have kids or a wet boyfriend like Robert or a fitted pine kitchen or a matching suite in the sitting room. She'd be like Alice; she'd travel light and free over tundra or desert or veldt, with just a toothbrush and a change of clothing.

Alice. Rowan unzipped a corner of her bag and poked inside until she felt the little parcel. No, Alice would never send a boring present.

* * *

Coming home across the garden several hours later, Rowan was pleased to see a light in the kitchen window. Bryony was home early! Rowan slammed the old wooden gate behind her and ran up the path. As she had foretold in the morning, it had been raining all day, and the overgrown shrubs each gave her an extra drenching as she brushed past them. At this time of the autumn afternoon, the garden was growing dark and a little creepy, with rustlings and scurryings among the wet leaves, so Rowan was glad to see the light, quite apart from the excitement of being able to show Bryony the parcel. She opened the back door, and in the tiny space of time between shoving it open a crack, and then all the way, she froze.

The shadow which loomed across the creamy kitchen wall was not that of her sister. In fact, it was like nothing so much as a child's nightmare impression of a witch, pointed chin and hooked nose almost meeting over a shrunken mouth. Rowan was aware of the damp outside air caught in her throat and the cold door-handle clutched between her rigid fingers. She tried to draw back, but the door continued to fall open, revealing her to the figure inside, and rather than be seen to retreat, she stepped bravely into the room.

Immediately the sinister shadow dwindled into that of a young man who was sitting slouched at the kitchen table, his feet, in well-worn trainers, stuck out into the middle of the floor. He had a straggly little red beard and was wearing a peaked cap which had, taken together, given the impression of a witch's profile. Beneath the cap, which was the ridiculous fleecy sort with earflaps, his lean, beaky face was chapped and freckled, as though he'd recently spent a lot of time out of doors.

'Hi,' he said casually, as Rowan hesitated upon her own doorstep. 'You must just be back from school, right?'

Well of course she was back from school, any idiot could tell that by her uniform and bag of books! This particular idiot had an American accent and he seemed to be breathing rather quickly and heavily for someone who was lounging back in a chair. It was almost as if he'd been interrupted in some task and had sat down to draw attention away from his activity. Rowan remained by the door, not wanting to cut off her escape, but with her eyes darting all over the kitchen. There was no obvious sign of disorder.

'So I guess you must be Rowan?'

Rowan should perhaps have been relieved that the stranger knew her name, but she wasn't. His knowledge didn't seem to transform him into a comfortable family friend, but just made his presence even creepier. Who was he? What else did he know about her?

'The door was open so I came right in.'

That was something which made sense. Petronella, already scatty and forgetful, had become worse and worse as her pregnancy advanced. Rowan turned automatically to look at the door and then back at the young man, who was smiling amiably and looking, in his jeans, baseball jacket and T-shirt, like nothing so much as – of course – a student.

'Are you looking for Robert?' she said, breathing out quickly in relief. Robert, whose real grown-up job was teaching at the university, occasionally brought students, and especially foreign students, home.

'Yeah.' The young man's smile widened into a grin, giving Rowan a glimpse of perfect American teeth flashing unexpectedly between the rusty fronds of his beard. 'I thought Dr Monteith might be home.' He stuck out his hand. 'Will McCantrip.'

It took Rowan a moment to realize that he was introducing himself and that she was supposed to advance and shake his outstretched hand. She did so reluctantly, somehow drawn despite herself across the expanse of polished floor. It wouldn't quite do to show him how very rude she thought he was. Perhaps in America students strolled into their tutors' houses all the time and made themselves at home whilst the family was out. So she said 'How do you do?' super-politely and touched his hand for as short a time as possible.

'Will Dr Monteith be much longer?'

'It's hard to say. He doesn't have a set time.' She wasn't going to have to make coffee for this pushy person and then chat to him until Robert turned up, was she? Rowan had retreated to the far end of the table the instant the handshake was over, instinctively keeping her distance. Will McCantrip didn't exactly look dangerous, but she wasn't taking any chances. And she particularly disliked the way in which he was peering at her through his little, round-rimmed glasses.

'Then perhaps I'd better be on my way. I just thought perhaps he did some of his work at home.'

'No, well, he has to go into the university for his lectures and seminars and what not.'

'The university, yeah, of course.'

Well *of course*, thought Rowan. Where else would a student expect to find their teacher? And if this Will McCantrip were really Robert's student, why didn't he go and see him in his office?

'So are you in one of Robert's classes?' she said.

'Well, that's the point. I missed the start of term. I had a bit of travelling to do in connection with family business so I was too late to sign up for this course I'm really keen to do. So when I couldn't find Dr Monteith at the university, I decided to drop by here and see whether I could make up the work I've missed.'

'You're really keen to do a class in economics?'

'Economics, sure.' Will looked at Rowan steadily as though he dared her to disbelieve him. Then, to her great relief, he began to get to his feet. 'But it looks like I'll need to leave it for another day.' He zipped up his jacket. 'Nice meeting you, Rowan. I'll just go out this way.' And he shrugged past her to the back door. Standing up, he wasn't as tall as she'd expected. Just a scruffy young man who'd come blundering in at the wrong time. Bit of a loser really. Yet, as he raised his hand to Rowan before disappearing into the night, she didn't really think so. There was something definitely odd about Mr Will McCantrip.

The moment he was out of sight, Rowan flung herself at the back door and locked it. Then she dashed through the house to the hall and checked the front door. Unlocked. So perhaps Will McCantrip was telling the truth?

Or perhaps he wasn't. Rowan's heart seemed to jerk right into her throat when she remembered all the beautiful jewellery – old pieces of his mother's – which Robert had given Petronella. Rowan flew straight up the stairs, one hand unconsciously clutching her breast like the heroine of one of Robert's novels. Reaching the front bedroom, she opened the top drawer of her mother's dressing-table – and nearly fainted with relief when she saw the stack of slim leather cases.

Just to be sure, she checked the contents, but everything was in place: the pearl pendant and earrings, the garnet bracelet, and the little snake of amethysts which lay so smoothly round Petronella's white throat. Rowan sank down onto the bed, only aware now of her trembling knees and rapid breathing. Nothing had been touched. So Will McCantrip was probably exactly what he said he was: one of Robert's students. But wait a minute. It was *she* who had said he was a student. She replayed the conversation in her head. *She* had asked if he were waiting for Robert, *she* had asked if he were in one of his classes, and Will McCantrip had simply agreed with her, and then left before Robert could come home and prove him a liar. How could she have been so stupid? But if Will didn't know Robert, *how did he know her name?* For a moment she almost stopped breathing, but then she forced herself to be sensible. He had found the door open, been snooping around the kitchen, seen something with her name on it and then, when she'd disturbed him, taken a chance on her being Rowan. That must be it.

Rowan jumped up, closed the drawer, and

ran back downstairs to the kitchen. There must be something here with her name on it. An envelope, a list, a dental appointment card. She riffled over the papers pinned to the family noticeboard: a flyer for Robert's reading, *Marjorie Gloaming, the controversial author, otherwise known as Dr Robert Monteith, will read from the latest Gloaming romance*, a note from Bryony's music-teacher, Mum's ante-natal clinic card – but nothing mentioning the existence of Ms Rowan Durwood. She dropped her hands to her sides and stood staring in disbelief round the pretty room with its floral curtains and touches of polished copper. Petronella always kept the house neat and tidy but now, fully possessed by the nesting instinct, she seemed to have tidied her younger daughter out of sight. The odd bits of paper, the letters and books and magazines which drifted onto the corners of the dresser or the window seat had all gone. There was nothing to tell the intruder that someone called Rowan lived here.

TWO

'What *are* you doing?' Bryony, who had let herself in at the front door, came padding up softly behind her.

Rowan screamed. 'Don't come sneaking up on me like that!'

'I wasn't sneaking. I was walking, ordinary walking, one foot after the other. But what were you doing? You were staring into space as though you'd been turned to stone. Playing statues?' Bryony, like a slim, scornful statue herself, black shiny jacket, black skirt and tights and trainers, black sculpted hair, looked disdainfully at her little sister.

'Look, Bryony, there's nothing in here with my name on it, is there?'

'What on earth are you getting at?'

'Mum's had a really big clean and tidy, hasn't she?'

'Yeah, well, but that's normal. Pregnant women always want to tidy the place up for the baby coming.'

'But she's done it really well, hasn't she? I mean, if you were a stranger and you walked in here, there's nothing to tell you that a girl called Rowan lives here, is there? No schoolbooks, no notes from the school – look, there's a letter from your clarsach teacher – but nothing about me.'

'I wouldn't worry about it, Rowan, I don't think Mum's trying to obliterate you. It just happens that you're not important enough to be on the noticeboard. Nothing ever happens to you.'

'No, no, you don't understand!' Rowan waved her hands wildly in her sister's face. 'Something has happened. When I came home this afternoon, the back door was open and there was a young man sitting right there at the table as though he owned the place!'

'What?' For once, Bryony's cool was jolted.

'Was Robert here? Had he let him in?'

'No, there was no-one here, that's the thing. I think Mum must've left the front door unlocked and he'd simply walked in and was trying his luck when I came and disturbed him. Nothing seems to be missing.'

'But what happened when you came in? Did he run for it?'

'No, that's what's so horrible.' Rowan wrapped her arms around herself. 'He sat there at the table as though he'd every right to be there and chatted to me and I just sort of found myself joining in. I asked him if he were waiting for Robert and he said he was, so I began thinking it was all right him being there and he was a student who didn't know it was rude in this country to just walk into houses. He was American.'

'So what else did he say?'

'Oh Bryony, I was so stupid!' Rowan hated admitting this to her scornful sister, but it was a relief to confess everything. 'I asked him if he went to one of Robert's classes and he just agreed with everything I said and told me a story about being late for enrolment and I believed him! And then he said he couldn't wait any longer and he shoved off.'

'But weren't you suspicious when you came in and found him here?'

'*Of course* I was suspicious, I'm not that thick, but the thing was, the thing was, Bryony, he knew my name.'

'Your name?' Bryony raised her plucked eyebrows so high that they lost themselves in the gelled tangle of her hair.

'He said "You must be Rowan".'

'So you thought Robert must've told him your name.'

'Yes. It was only after he'd left that I realized that I was the one who'd mentioned Robert to him. So then I thought, perhaps he wasn't one of Robert's students, perhaps he was a burglar who'd sneaked in and seen my name on something – but there's nothing here with my name on it!'

'So that just makes it more likely that he really is one of Robert's nerdy students.' Bryony put her jacket over the back of a chair and picked up the kettle. 'Want some tea?'

'I suppose it does.' Rowan automatically fetched the biscuit tin from the cupboard. 'It just seems such a weird thing to do, walking right into a stranger's house.'

'Did you say he was American?' Bryony, who had filled the kettle, switched it on.

'Yes. He said his name was Will McCantrip.'

'McCantrip?' Bryony wrinkled up her nose, in which a small silver ring glittered. 'What an odd name. It sounds Scottish though, his family must've emigrated from here.'

'And now perhaps he lives in one of these homey little towns where everyone knows one another and they all walk in and out of each others' houses all day long.'

'Perhaps.' Bryony, who didn't usually talk so much, was relapsing into her normal, one-word answers.

'So maybe I'm making a fuss about nothing.' Rowan nibbled miserably at a chocolate biscuit. The stranger's appearance had altered the whole balance of her life. If someone could just walk into your safe kitchen, who knows what other awful things could happen?

'Here.' Bryony pushed a mug of tea across the kitchen table, and then sat down herself. 'Perhaps this will teach Mum to keep the door locked.'

'Oh don't tell her! She'll make such a fuss.

I'm sure we'll never see him again.' But even as she spoke she shuddered.

Then she remembered why she'd been running so eagerly across the garden towards the lighted window. 'Bryony, I forgot! Something else happened today!' Rowan fetched her bag, rummaged inside, and dropped the package triumphantly on the table. 'Look at that.'

'What on earth—?'

'*Where* on earth's more like it. Look at the stamps and postmark!'

Just as Rowan had done that morning, Bryony felt the parcel all over and peered at the stamps, although she stopped short at sniffing it.

'Alice! Alice must've sent us a present. Fancy her remembering us.' Rowan almost squeaked with enthusiasm. She could hardly believe that the mighty Alice would remember them from one brief meeting.

Bryony, however, remained irritatingly cool. 'Why didn't you open it in the morning?'

'But it's addressed to both of us!'

'You didn't need to wait for me.'

To think she could've opened it straight

away instead of spending a whole frustrating day longing for tea-time!

'I thought you'd be cross.'

'I'm not a *baby*, you know. And it probably isn't anything special.'

'I know *that*,' said Rowan, trying to be cool in her turn. 'I just thought it was nice of her, that's all.'

'Go on then, you open it.' Bryony pushed the package across the table, her black varnished nails glistening on her slim white hand.

'I'll need scissors.' Rowan jumped up, fetched them, and sat down again, trying to control her excitement in the face of her sister's calm superiority. She sawed through the thick string and the paper unfolded itself, revealing two further twists of a thinner, dark yellow paper and a third object which was wrapped in a piece of soft leather.

'Look, this is for you.'

Bryony's name was pencilled on one of the twists. Rowan watched eagerly as her sister opened it. Bryony's face was studiously blank, but then, despite herself, her eyes lit up as a silver ring fell onto her hand.

'It's a nose-ring, a really good one.' Much bigger than the one she already wore, the ring was set with an amber bead. 'That really is quite cool. Well done, Alice.'

Rowan felt vindicated. Her heroine had actually made Bryony express admiration.

'Your turn.'

Rowan unfolded the other screw of yellow paper. Whatever lay inside was light and very small.

'So what is it?' Bryony craned across the table.

'I don't know yet.' Rowan picked open the final fold and a tiny white seal emerged. The little beast had been carved from some white substance, ivory or bone, and every detail was perfect, from flipper to smiling whisker. 'It's so beautiful!'

'Looks like it's been made of some sort of *tooth*,' said Bryony.

'I wonder who made it? And where does it come from?' In her imagination, Rowan could see a squat, fur-clad figure working away at the bit of ivory whilst the flickering oil-lamp lit up an igloo's icy walls.

'There's something written on the inside

of the wrapping-paper—' Bryony tilted the paper and the remaining package slid onto the table. Heavier than the other two gifts, it chinked slightly as it moved.

'What does it say?'

'It's written in pencil.'

The scrawl was difficult to decipher on the brown paper, but by holding it up to the light, the girls read: 'Picked up these pressies for you in Siberia and Alaska, which is where I am right now. The other thing is for your mother, but not until she marries Robert. Long story. Love, Alice.'

Rowan and Bryony looked at one another, and then at the leather-wrapped object.

'Alice, Woman of Mystery,' said Bryony. 'You open it.'

The moment she'd picked it up, Rowan realized that the leather was the source of the smell. 'It smells all fishy and peculiar.' What on earth could Alice be sending to her ex-husband's girlfriend? Suddenly Rowan felt reluctant to unroll the package, but she couldn't let Bryony know that. 'OK then,' she said, and tipped the contents of the leather wrapper onto the table.

An oval gold medallion on a slender chain lay before their startled eyes, its colour richer and sweeter than that of the bleached pine boards.

For a moment, neither girl could speak.

The object's surface was enamelled with tiny, vivid flowers. The centre-piece was a rose, and around it rambled all the flowers which you might find in a cottage garden – pansies, lilies, daisies and sweetpeas. And each blossom was as perfect as its lifesize self would be.

'Alice got this in *Alaska*?' Rowan's voice was an awed whisper.

'And for Mum – but not until she and Robert get married! Who knows when that'll be?'

'Oh rats, of course, you left before the post,' groaned Rowan. 'Well, I've got news for you.' She leant over and stroked the medallion very gently with one finger. The gold felt very slightly warm, despite its long imprisonment in oily leather and thick brown paper. 'Mum might just be wearing this sooner than you think.'

'What on earth do you mean?' Bryony's eyes blazed up briefly behind her glasses which, like Will McCantrip's, were small and round.

Rowan sighed dramatically. 'Robert's divorce papers arrived this morning. Now there's nothing to stop him and Mum from getting married.'

'But Mum's pregnant!'

'It sounded like she meant to get married before the baby's born.'

'That is just terminally uncool.'

'Yeah.'

'You know why she's doing this?' Bryony had become almost talkative in her disgust. 'If she got married *after* the baby was born, she wouldn't be the centre of attention. Everyone would be huffing round the baby, saying how sweet it was, rather than round her, saying didn't she make a lovely bride?'

'Yeah.' Rowan hated to agree with Bryony, but she was right. Mum was at her happiest when surrounded by admirers. 'And there's worse to come. She wants us to be bridesmaids.'

'Non-negotiable.'

'Ladies-in-waiting, she actually said.'

'Get to Falkirk! There is absolutely, totally, completely no way in which I am going to get tarted-up as a maid, lady, wench or waiting-person of any description whatsoever!'

Rowan was impressed. She hadn't heard her sister use so many words in one sentence since they'd moved into Dryburgh Place.

'Tell Mum, not me. I'm sure I heard the front door.'

'Hide the present!'

Rowan bundled the medallion back into its leather coat and was shoving the whole thing into her bag just as Petronella came tripping into the kitchen.

'You're both home, girls, good.'

Petronella was wearing a cloak with a fake-fur collar and her blond hair was done up in a thick plait. Since she'd become pregnant she had dressed, Rowan thought, more and more like the mother in a fairy story. Today, for example, when she took off the cloak, she revealed a long embroidered smock.

'I'm exhausted. Where do you think I've been?'

'Not teaching your old acting ladies?' said Rowan warily.

'That's tomorrow. Bryony, did Rowan tell you the great news?' Petronella looked very slightly uncomfortable as she said this. Everyone knew that Bryony could be quite frightening when she disapproved of something.

'If you mean about Robert's divorce, yes she did.' Bryony got up and, going over to the mirror, began to change the ring already in her nose for the new one.

'Isn't it wonderful? It means that your new little brother or sister won't be born out of wedlock.'

'Oh *Mum*,' said Bryony, in a tone which should have warned Petronella to change the subject.

'Not if we get married straight away, that is, I've just been to the Register Office and then—'

Rowan couldn't bear to hear another happy word.

'Look at this, Mum,' she said, pushing her little seal across the table. 'Alice sent us some stuff. It came this morning.'

'Oh. Cute.' Diverted, Petronella picked up the carving. 'And where might *her ladyship* be now?'

Petronella did not like Alice.

'Alaska, she says.'

Petronella inspected the seal more closely. 'I suppose this is an Inuit carving then. Sea-lion's tusk or something. Quite sweet but rather primitive.'

'I like it,' said Rowan, taking back her present and tucking it firmly into her pocket. 'And it was nice of her to remember us.'

'I don't suppose it cost her much to send you a bit of old tooth – Bryony, what's that horrible thing through your nose?'

Bryony had turned round from the mirror, the heavy ring lending a barbaric gleam to her neat features.

'From Alice. Good, yeah?'

Petronella wrinkled up *her* small nose in disdain. 'You're not actually going to wear that thing, are you?'

'Sure.'

'Well don't tell Robert where it came from, you know how he feels about Alice.'

'No problem.'

'I really mean it. Don't tell Robert—'

'What am I not to be told?' Robert had appeared in their midst, treading silently in his expensive Italian shoes. His new family whirled around, regarding his tall, handsome figure with varying degrees of guilt.

'Sweetheart, you're early! Kiss, kiss!' Petronella stood on tiptoe to embrace her beloved.

'Petronella, you haven't tired yourself out gallivanting, have you? Sit down and I'll make you some camomile tea.'

As Petronella subsided gracefully into a chair, Robert regarded the girls sternly. 'And what am I not to know?'

How unfair to be cross with them, and not Mum, thought Rowan. Typical. She sighed and said sullenly, 'Alice sent us some stuff. From Alaska.' She was beginning to wish that Alice hadn't bothered. The gifts had caused nothing but trouble.

'Alice? Alaska?' Robert's noble features paled. Any mention of his terrifying ex-wife alarmed him. 'What exactly did she send?'

'This.' Bryony turned to face him, her dark eyes daring him to say what he really thought.

'Er, very unusual. Rowan?'

'This wee seal, isn't it gorgeous?' Rowan held it out to Robert, who actually picked it up and regarded it closely.

'Inuit, I suppose. Good heavens, these objects are usually pretty pricey.'

Rowan smiled in secret triumph. Alice had

sent her a really expensive present, not a miserable bit of old tooth. And when Robert and Petronella eventually saw the wonderful gold medallion, then they'd know how generous Alice really was. Not many ex-wives would buy their successor something so magnificent.

'Give it back to Rowan, darling, and listen, I've got so much to tell you!' Petronella waved her delicate hands with commanding grace.

'Petronella, your tea!' Robert switched on the kettle and began fussing with herbal tea-bags and honey.

'I went straight to the Registrar's to see about the marriage licence, and the wedding's going to have to be on a weekday. It's such short notice that all the Saturdays are booked – but you won't mind missing school, will you, poppets? – and then I went to that wonderful dressmaker in the Royal Mile and she's going to run me up something in time. After all, I can hardly expect to buy a readymade wedding dress when I'm this shape, can I?' Mum laughed merrily. 'And I'm taking you girls there on Saturday morning. I know I can't tempt you out of your beloved black, Bryony, so I thought a nice dark top and a long silk skirt in one of the more sombre tartans, and something similar for you, Rowan – and you'll wear the kilt, won't you, darling? A dress kilt with one of those gorgeous velvet doublets, a Prince Charlie, isn't that what it's called? With ruffles?'

Her victims looked at Petronella with horror and disbelief.

Robert was the first to splutter out a reply. 'But I haven't worn a kilt since I was at school!'

'And a shocking waste too! You've got the perfect figure for a kilt.'

'But we agreed that this was going to be an informal occasion. My Armani would do splendidly.'

'But I've set my heart on a sweet little Scottish wedding.' Tears sparkled in Mum's blue eyes. 'And you could play your clarsach, Bryony.'

'I'm not playing my clarsach and I'm not wearing a tartan skirt.' Bryony picked up her bag and marched out of the room.

'Robert, you'd look *so* wonderful.'

Poor Robert. Rowan actually felt sorry for him. He didn't have one single hope of wearing his lovely new suit on his wedding day. She and Bryony were getting off lightly by comparison. At least they wouldn't have to show their knees.

'I'm not sure about the doublet, Petronella, I think they're for evening wear only. I'd probably have the Lord Lyon Knight-at-Arms down on me if I wore one during the day.'

'But you will wear the kilt, won't you, darling, dearest Robert?'

'If you don't think I'll look silly?'

'When did you *ever* look silly?'

Oh yuk. Rowan followed her sister's example and escaped upstairs. If she got a chance later, she could ask Robert if Will McCantrip were really one of his students. That would be one weight off her mind.

She opened the door to her own pretty room and went inside. Like the rest of Robert's house, Petronella had redecorated it when they moved in with him and the new Swedish furniture and fluffy rugs were all Rowan had ever wanted. Now she even had her own computer, a Christmas present from Robert. She didn't suppose she could blame him for wanting to make money as a best-selling novelist, especially as some of that money was coming her way, but that didn't stop him from being the silliest grown-up she'd ever met. But at least she and Bryony had persuaded him to write a more sensible book this time. Although she wouldn't admit it to Mum, she was almost looking forward to Friday's reading. In a way, it would be her triumph as much as Robert's.

Rowan sank down into her rocking chair, taking Alice's present from her pocket. She rubbed her finger along the smooth ivory. In a few years, she too would be travelling the world, sending back presents to her little brother or sister. And when Mum saw Alice's lovely gift, she wouldn't think so badly of her.

Even the wedding might be fun.

Things weren't so bad when you got used to them.

And then she remembered coming into her kitchen and seeing Will McCantrip sprawled there, perfectly at home, and shivered.

THREE

Lady Maisie McNeil awoke with as much of a jolt as it was possible for a ghost to experience. Like all phantoms, she was perfectly accustomed to finding herself in unexpected places, and was confident that in a few moments she would discover what psychic reason had drawn her to this particular spot.

Her discomfort was due to the fact that she was drifting between tiers of books. During her short and dashing life, Lady Maisie had had little time for literature, so to find herself surrounded by thousands of volumes gave her the stifled feeling of being trapped in the schoolroom when she longed to be galloping across the moors. And there were far more books here than had ever graced the barren shelves of Clachanfeckle Castle.

The ghost floated, cross and disconsolate, between the rows. What on earth, or under heaven, had brought her here? She had fallen into a refreshing slumber on the beautiful banks of Loch Rannoch and now she was in this loathsome stuffy place where, from the far end of the room, someone was speaking in a loud and pompous voice, as though addressing a crowd.

But wait! Lady Maisie knew those fiendish tones only too well! Gathering up her invisible silk skirts, the ghost skirled down the chamber, tartan plaid and long curls flying. Yes, it was just as she feared: there stood her mortal enemy, the monstrous Monteith, a ridiculous necktie wound around his silly throat, calmly speaking to a large company of dowagers and dames.

The ghost clenched her slender fists in fury. She thought that Rowan had stopped Monteith from writing lies about her, yet here he was, spouting on about her beloved Clachanfeckle!

'"Clachanfeckle is ours!" cried one of the redcoats from the topmost battlement.

'"Aye, but at what terrible cost!" groaned James Arbuthnot, staggering back against the wall of the spiral stair, one hand clutching the breast of his red tunic, the other still holding his bloody sword. "I am dishonoured for ever. I have slain a woman."'

Lady Maisie sank down onto one of the despised bookcases, clutching her own lace-frilled bosom.

'At his feet lay the body of a beautiful woman, her long skirts kilted up, her lovely hair still covered by her loosened plaid, and in her hand a heavy claymore. Just a moment before she had been slashing savagely at Arbuthnot, and he, mistaking her in the smoke which swirled around them for a kilted Highlander, had stabbed her through the heart.

'"I would have stayed my hand had I known my valiant adversary was a woman, even had it been my own death!" cried the heartbroken soldier. "What have I done?"

'"You have slain Lady Maisie McNeil, the flower o' Rannoch!" keened a voice from

48

the stair behind him. "May the curse of the house of McNeil fall upon you!"

'An aged crone in tartan rags pushed past the weeping officer and flung herself down beside the lovely corpse. "Och, my lassie, my bonnie nursling!"'

There was a murmur of tearful appreciation from Robert's audience. Hankies were touched to powdered cheeks and permed grey heads bobbed and nodded. Lady Maisie's eyes also filled with tears. Monteith had kept his word to the child, and now the whole world would know how she, Lady Maisie McNeil, had lived and died as a true Scottish heroine. The ghost's thin, spectral blood almost ran warm with pride, and leaping up from her bookcase, she danced a wild reel over the heads of the audience. She polka'd with such vigour that hands were raised to tuck in straying curls or to turn up collars against the sudden draught.

Then, panting, the ghost sat herself down, and as Robert continued to read, she looked around for his family. Yes, there was that frippery hizzie, his sweetheart, now big with child. Only to be expected, the ghost thought.

She'd had no time herself for such nonsense. And there was the black-clad miss, with a horrid ring through her nose, like a bull about to be led to market, doubtless a foolish latter-day fad – unless the girl had committed some crime, and the ring was the mark of the felon. And yes, there was the little Rowan creature. Grown a trifle since last she'd seen her, but still a scrap of a lassie with her big eyes and mousy hair. And still wearing a shapeless, long-sleeved bodice over her blue trews. Those trousers, however, Lady Maisie admired. If only she'd been able to fight, like a man, in breeks, rather than cumbered by skirts, she might never have received her death blow.

However, as she watched Rowan, Lady Maisie saw the child start upright in her seat, eyes staring, almost in fact as though she'd seen a ghost. Automatically, Lady Maisie checked herself for visibility. It was many years since she'd been powerful enough to come into plain sight, and she was certain that she remained unseen. The child must have been frightened by something else. The ghost followed Rowan's gaze and saw that the person at whom she was staring with such horror was a shabby, bearded young man wearing a foppish furred hat with a long peak drawn down over his face. What was so alarming about him? He was slumped in the back row, rather out of place amongst the mainly elderly women, but scarcely sinister. Curious, the ghost allowed herself to drift down in his direction – and no sooner was she within the young man's orbit than she found her nose twitching and her ears buzzing.

There was mischief in the air.

Not the playful pranks of a poltergeist, nor the cruel menace of a ghoul, but something more human and less comprehensible. Something which smelt, to Lady Maisie, of plots hatched over sloppy bowls of porridge, something tangled yet yearning, and something which the child, like herself, had picked up on. Observing him, Lady Maisie saw that he was watching Rowan from under the peak of his ugly cap, his bearded lips curved into a half-smile. Without a doubt, this man was dangerous – and dangerous to the very lass who had saved Lady Maisie's good name from Monteith's folly! All the ghost's loyal feelings surged to her breast. Would the woman who had given her life for

Prince Charlie stand aside when her own preserver was in danger? Never! Although she might be a little inconvenienced by her ghostly status, Lady Maisie was determined to stop at nothing to protect Rowan and her family from whatever threat the mysterious young man represented.

Lady Maisie was right. Rowan was horrified to see Will McCantrip. One moment she'd been lolling in her plastic chair, allowing Robert's deep, tuneful voice to drift past her – and the next she was sitting bolt upright, her spine as straight and cold as an icicle.

What was Will doing here? How did he know about the reading? He hadn't – awful thought – followed her? She wished now that she'd asked Robert if he knew him, but once her alarm had faded, she hadn't wanted to make a fuss. Rowan turned to nudge her sister, but as she did so, over a hundred pairs of hands rose from their owners' woollen or polyester laps and clapped fervently.

'Absolutely fascinating!' 'And such a young, handsome man!' 'I'd no idea so much research went into his work.'

All round Rowan, the women were commenting favourably on Robert's work, appearance and charm.

'Anyone who would like a signed copy—' The words of the bookshop's representative, a pretty young woman in T-shirt and jeans, were drowned by the rustle of credit cards being withdrawn from purses and the soft thud of sensible shoes advancing across the carpet towards Robert.

'Bryony, he's here, look, Will McCantrip!' Rowan clutched her sister's elbow to prevent herself being swept away by the tide of literary enthusiasts.

'Where?'

'Over there, at the back.'

But Will's chair was empty.

'He's gone.' Had she imagined his presence? Rowan remembered the strange sensation of being haunted which had oppressed her the previous year. Surely it wasn't coming back? But Will McCantrip wasn't a ghost. She had actually touched his horrible, sweaty hand. Rowan looked around wildly. The women were forming an eager but orderly queue in front of the desk at which Robert sat, pen in hand, a glossy tower of novels by his side. Then she turned towards where she had last seen Petronella – and froze. If Rowan's spine had been an icicle of dread before, now her entire body must be an iceberg!'

Mum was talking to Will McCantrip! And not just talking, but chatting and laughing as though he were an absolutely entrancing old friend. She stood with her cloak thrown back and her head graciously inclined towards Will, whilst the young man, who had actually removed his cap, stood grinning before her.

For a moment, Rowan could only watch. Then, suppressing an urge to run to her mother and hustle her out of the room, she sneaked up to stand behind Will.

'And so your family came originally from Scotland?' Mum was saying. 'That is so fascinating.'

'It was a long time ago. The seventeenth century, in fact.'

'Good heavens, your ancestors must've been on the *Mayflower*!'

'No, ma'am,' said Will respectfully. 'The Pilgrim Fathers were English. My family sailed from Glasgow to Virginia. The tobacco trade.'

'Virginia! How romantic!'

'You haven't been to America recently yourself, have you, ma'am?' There was a curious intensity in Will's words.

'Oh goodness me, no! I'm not doing any travelling at the moment!' Petronella laughed gaily and glanced meaningfully at the folds of her smock.

A blush spread over Will's sandy features. 'Oh uh, sure, Mrs Monteith, of course not.'

'And I'm not Mrs Monteith – or not yet anyway. Just call me Petronella.'

Will looked even hotter. 'Ah sure, yeah, thank you. But your little girl here, she's Rowan, right?'

Little girl indeed! Rowan bristled.

'Yes, certainly. Rowan, Will tells me he called at the house the other day. Why didn't you tell me? He's one of Robert's students.'

'Well, hoping to be.' Will smiled, showing his white teeth. 'Nice to see you again, Rowan. I remembered seeing that poster about Dr Monteith's reading in your kitchen, so I just decided to come along. And I'm sure glad I did.' He bowed his head chivalrously to Petronella.

Rowan – Will's eyes upon her – was speechless.

'Now, Will, you must come to supper. We

must show you some traditional Scottish hospitality.'

'I certainly would enjoy that, Petronella. I'd just love to visit your beautiful home again.'

Rowan didn't know what there was about Will's words to make her shiver.

'Mum,' she said, 'you shouldn't be standing about. Perhaps we shouldn't wait for Robert but go home now.'

Petronella beamed. 'Why, darling, that's so thoughtful, but I couldn't possibly go without Robert. Will, I'm so busy next week, but why don't you come on Friday evening? About six. You know the way?'

He certainly does, thought Rowan.

'And then you can meet – why there he is, finished already, darling?'

'Petronella, what are you doing on your feet?' Unconsciously echoing Rowan, Robert, splendidly dressed in dark suit, velvet waistcoat and gleaming silk cravat, had come up to them. 'It really is time I took you home.'

And what about Bryony and me? thought Rowan. I suppose we could take the bus or even walk for all you care.

'Robert, you must've met Will McCantrip,

he's one of your new students. From Virginia, the Virginia McCantrips, Scottish originally, so exciting!' And Petronella bestowed smiles right and left upon sweetheart and new admirer.

'McCantrip, of course!'

To Rowan's disbelief, Robert strode forward and shook Will's limp hand in a hearty, manly fashion. 'Now you must be the chap who applied for my course on Economic History. I'm afraid you're a bit late, but if you drop into my office, we can discuss it.'

So Will had been speaking the truth! He *had* registered for one of Robert's classes. But why didn't Rowan feel reassured?

'Are your fans really prepared to let you go so soon?' said Petronella.

Robert was making ushing movements towards the staircase. 'I think I've given them their money's worth,' he said complacently. 'And you ought to be at home with your feet up.'

'Then we'll see you on Friday, Will, six-ish. I really feel our meeting like this was *meant*,' declared Petronella.

'And do you know, Petronella, so do I,' said Will.

Rowan shivered again.

'Come *along*, Petronella,' urged Robert. 'Tomorrow morning, Will, my office. I'll be there from eleven. Now, girls.'

Bryony, who'd been lurking behind a display of sci-fi, slouched forward, and she and Rowan followed Robert as he shepherded Petronella down the staircase and out into the wet Edinburgh night.

FOUR

Will's meeting with Petronella and her family had not gone unobserved. Lady Maisie, perched upon the Media Studies section, had been watching with increasing concern. The ghost couldn't put her phantom finger upon what exactly was wrong with the young man, but all of her psychic instincts told her that he was not the eager-to-please young student he pretended to be. Behind his smiling face lurked a devious spirit. But what exactly did he want? And why did Lady Maisie feel that there was something very slightly familiar about him? And the images which she picked up from his thoughtwaves were similarly confusing. Above all there was a craving. Will might be smiling and chatting politely, but behind his innocent blue eyes, his mind was on fire with longing – but longing for what?

When Rowan and her family had left, Will lingered to buy a copy of *Bluff Your Way in Economics* and then, he, too, made his way outside. Lady Maisie took off from her shelf and followed in his wake. Pausing only to zip up his jacket against the rain, Will crossed the main road and set off uphill towards the castle.

Lady Maisie had haunted Edinburgh frequently since her untimely death and it always gladdened her ghostly heart to find the Old Town so unchanged since her last visit as a mortal. Yes, there were the very cobblestones over which she used to run so lightheartedly when returning from a night of dancing to her Aunt Janet's apartment in the leaning tenements of Gladstone's Land.

But this was no time for sentiment. Will had turned down the High Street away from the castle and then, beyond the cathedral, he turned again, plunging into a close so narrow that he could have touched both walls at once with his outstretched hands. It was a wet, moonless night, and the lanterns which now cast their mysteriously steady light over the Old Town outlined the towering buildings, making their turrets and gables look as romantically insubstantial as Lady Maisie herself.

Further and further into the dark alleys went Will until, at the foot of a particularly dank close, he stopped, unlocked a door, and vanished into an even thicker darkness.

He did not, naturally, disappear from Lady Maisie's sight. The ghost sailed through the door and ahead of him up the stone stair. The building was derelict, and whilst the lower floors showed signs of restoration – wheelbarrows, sacks of plaster and work-men's tools lay everywhere – the upper were untouched. Will ascended slowly, lighting his way with a small torch he'd brought from his pocket, whilst Lady Maisie, zooming ahead, unerringly found the one door with a new lock. Giving a wild Gaelic war-cry, the ghost bounded clean through the sturdy wooden panels, and eddying once or twice around the room within, settled down to await the arrival of her prey.

It took Will several panting minutes to catch up with his unseen companion. The ghost sneered as he wheezed his way across the room. In her mortal days, she could have run up every one of the stairs and still have had the strength to despatch an enemy with one blow of her claymore!

Having lit a couple of candles, Will sank down upon the single chair, took off his cap, and mopped his face with it. Despite his panting, he was grinning, a deeply satisfied grin.

Then he got up, went over to the upended wooden crate which served as a cupboard, and pulled out a narrow wooden box.

Ghost though she was, Lady Maisie felt the hairs rise on the back of her lovely neck. A box of that shape could, in her experience, contain only one thing.

But surely not? This handless mischief-maker could never— Will raised the lid, fumbled inside, and to the ghost's utter astonishment did, indeed, pull forth a set of Highland bagpipes. Lady Maisie sank down onto the window-sill. When Will had told Petronella that his family were Scottish, the ghost had taken it for a black lie. Not even a lifetime spent in the Americas could have given him such an uncouth tongue. Yet it seemed that he had spoken the truth. As she watched, Will slung the drones over his shoulder, squeezed the tartan bag beneath his oxter, and began to tune up, making all the unmelodious wailing with which Lady Maisie had once been so familiar.

How well she remembered the evenings in the great hall of Clachanfeckle Castle, her father and his clansmen quaffing claret by the roaring fire and old Rory pacing the chamber, the skirl of his pipes moving the company from memories of the joys of battle to tears for the fallen.

And now this miserable upstart was wheezing into the ancient instrument of war! Lady Maisie could barely contain herself. In her time no rascally Virginian tobacco merchant would have dared lay a finger on a chanter – but in the very act of whirling down upon Will, disguised as an icy draught, the phantom checked herself.

The young man's playing was not unskilful. Certainly he was far from having Rory's way of turning a phrase so sweetly that it stilled the heart, but the lad was a deal better than the tinkers who played for bawbees in the city's thoroughfares.

Now he was striding up and down his garret, blowing lustily, and producing a fine old march which the ghost knew well. Despite herself, Lady Maisie's satin-shod toes twitched to the rhythm. Could a lad who played the pipes really be a dastardly villain? Reaching the far side of the chamber, Will turned and advanced into the candlelight, his fox-coloured beard and ponytail brightening, and in that instant, Lady Maisie knew whom he resembled. She was transported back to a ball at the Old Assembly Rooms, herself the centre of a throng of beaux, and amongst them was just such a rusty-headed, beaknosed, skinnymalink of a McCantrip!

Lady Maisie had heard Will announce himself as a McCantrip, but misled by his wretched costume and drawling speech, she had never considered for a moment that he might be a genuine member of that noble house. But now, seeing his face by candlelight, just as his ancestor's had been two hundred and fifty years ago, Lady Maisie realized that she had been wrong.

No matter what evil he intended towards

Rowan and her family, he was indeed a member of an ancient line, and ought thus to command Lady Maisie's loyalty just as much as did the little girl. Had not a McCantrip died with her father in defence of Bonnie Prince Charlie? But the wee Rowan creature had saved the honour of the McNeils when she'd prevented Monteith from writing his foolish book!

Lady Maisie stamped her feet soundlessly in frustration. Even the most well-intentioned of ghosts could not act when the way ahead was as murky as an unlit close.

'For heaven's sake, Rowan, Will McCantrip was telling the truth! He *is* one of Robert's students. Or at least wants to be.' Bryony, who was removing her make-up, glared into her bedroom mirror at Rowan, who was standing behind her.

The family had arrived home an hour earlier, and after hot chocolate and biscuits and a great deal of Petronella telling Robert how wonderful he had been at the reading, Rowan had gone to bed. She couldn't, however, settle down and had gone to talk to Bryony.

Bryony did not encourage visitors – or at least, family visitors – and her room was not, Rowan thought, either comfortable or welcoming. Black walls and ceiling, with touches of silver, formed a backdrop to posters of Bryony's idols, rock stars whose pallid faces were pierced with jewellery far heavier than Alice's amber ring and sorrowful divas with long, lank hair. Rowan did not find them cheerful company, but this evening she ignored them for the sake of talking to Bryony.

'But he could've gone back to the university after he'd seen me and then registered for Robert's class!'

'But why bother? Just to get into our house?'

'I don't know why, but I think he did.'

'Rubbish. Lots of people come to Edinburgh to study. And after all, Robert is a famous economist.'

'But Bryony, you saw Will for yourself, he's so manky!'

'Just because he's a bit grubby doesn't mean he's evil.'

Bryony leant towards the mirror, patting around her eyes with cleansing cream. Seeing her sister's real face emerge from its usual mask of liner, shadow and mascara, gave Rowan an odd, painful feeling. She never seemed to see the old Bryony any more. Only occasionally, like now, or when Bryony was playing her clarsach.

'There's just something peculiar about him.'

'But what does it matter? We don't have to see him.'

'Yes we do. He's coming to supper next week.'

'So what's one supper?'

'But if he comes once, he'll come again.' Rowan didn't know how she knew this, but she did.

'Why should he? What's so special about coming here? We should just be thankful Mum didn't ask him to the wedding.' Bryony swabbed her face with a tissue.

'Bryony, what do you think about Mum marrying Robert?'

'I don't think anything.'

'But don't you think it'll make a difference?'

'You keep asking me what I *think*. I don't think anything about this McCantrip person,

and I don't think anything about Mum fling-
ing herself into matrimony.' Bryony smoothed
a fresh layer of cream over her face. For
someone who was above common thinking,
she took a great deal of care over her beauty
routine.

'OK. Remain brain-dead.'

Pleased that, for once, she'd had the last
word, Rowan returned to her own room. But
not to sleep. First, she took the mysterious gift
from its hiding place at the bottom of her
jewellery box, unwrapped the oily leather,
and let the chain trickle onto her hand,
followed by the small, solid weight of the
medallion. How had Alice found something so
delicate in the snowy wilderness? And why
was she giving it to Mum, who was, after all,
about to marry her ex-husband?

Rowan sat down on the bed. Two mysteries
in one week. Alice's unexplained present;
and the arrival of the untrustworthy Will
McCantrip. Why couldn't life just be smooth
and ordinary? A new baby and a wedding
were quite enough excitement without a
sinister visitor poking about in their lives.

The rocking chair creaked sharply, and
Rowan jumped. That hadn't happened since

last year's haunted summer. Surely she wasn't going to start dreaming again about a woman in long petticoats who slipped ahead of her round every corner?

Rowan scuttled across the room and stowed the medallion back in its hiding place. Then she took Mr Bear from his place of honourable retirement on the window-sill, and, leaping into bed, huddled well down under the duvet.

The chair creaked again, but very faintly, and this time, Rowan found the noise oddly comforting. It almost felt as though she were not alone with all her cares.

FIVE

'Hey, it's Drusilla the vampire,' said Rowan, entering the kitchen the next morning.

Bryony, who was wearing purple lipstick, a black lycra top, a black skirt with a slit up the side and high-heeled black boots didn't bother to reply.

'Mum's dressmaker's going to be really inspired by that goth look. Perhaps you can scare her into giving up the whole tartan dress idea.'

'I am not wearing a tartan dress.'

'But your mother did say just a tartan skirt with a dark top,' said Robert, looking anxious.

He dipped his croissant into his coffee. He was scheduled to go to the kiltmaker's whilst his womenfolk were fitted for their dresses.

'And dark it had better be,' said Bryony menacingly. 'You can get yourself dolled-up in ruffles, Robert, but not me.'

'I must admit I don't quite see myself as the ruffly type.' Robert was wearing chinos and a navy silk sweater. 'But I've got plans, girls. I won't let Petronella down.'

'Good for you.' Rowan was making herself tea and toast and marmalade, unaware that another presence, roosting upon the dresser, had raised her tired head at the sharp smell of oranges.

For a moment Lady Maisie forgot her weariness and remembered the happy days when she and her faithful old cook would make enough marmalade to last Clachanfeckle Castle for an entire year. And here was the lassie still eating the stuff two hundred and fifty years later!

Unaware of her place in the noble breakfast traditions of her country, Rowan spread her toast and sat down. 'C'mon, Bry, it won't be that bad. It's just to please Mum. And no-one's going to see you. I mean, no-one apart

71

from Mollie and people, and they don't count for clothes. And Robert's worse off, he's got to show his knees.'

'Don't be too sure about that,' Robert smiled mysteriously. 'More coffee, Bryony? I really think this Colombian's best for the morning, don't you?'

'Wonderful news!' Petronella surged into the room, her mobile in one hand, a pile of bridal magazines in the other. 'Mollie just called with the most marvellous suggestion. She's offered to lend us the Moated Grange for the wedding! Just think, if it's a nice day, we can get married in the garden.'

Rowan almost felt a small surge of excitement herself. Mollie, Mum's oldest friend, lived in a beautiful house by the river, and the sisters had spent many happy afternoons there when they were little, paddling or playing hide and seek in the orchard.

'That's an extraordinarily generous offer,' said Robert, looking equally pleased.

'The garden will be a perfect setting!'

'Unless it keeps raining, in which case you'll have to get married in a boat.'

'Bryony, don't be such a wet blanket! I'm

convinced it'll be a lovely day, autumn leaves, the last roses, the distant sound of the waterfall—'

'It'll be bari,' said Rowan, to make up for Bryony's lack of enthusiasm.

'Thank you, Rowan. Now we mustn't be late. Girls, remember you'll have to take your things off for Chantal to measure you. You are wearing clean undies, aren't you, Rowan?'

'Yes. And as you can see, Bryony definitely isn't wearing a vest, so you don't need to worry about her either.'

Bryony threw a crust at Rowan.

'And as for you, Bryony,' said Petronella, 'you needn't think you're getting away with that make-up at my wedding. Or that horrid ring.'

Rowan threw the crust back.

'Girls, now you're just being silly. Come along, Robert's going to drop us off.' Mum was now standing impatiently by the door. 'And why are you staring round the room like that, Rowan?'

'Just checking you'd locked up.' What if Will McCantrip came sneaking back whilst they were out?

'Of course I've locked up! I may be going a *little* bonkers by now—' Mum patted her bulge. '– but not all the way.'

'That's what you think,' said Rowan, but under her breath. Let Mum go on living in her dreamworld.

Fifteen minutes later, four people – or five, counting Lady Maisie – were crammed into the dressmaker's studio. The ghost felt much more at home than she had done at the terrible bookstore. Much as she had loved riding and hunting, she had still revelled in beautiful clothes, and the highlight of her visits to Edinburgh had been the sessions with Mistress Moultrie. The old dressmaker had behaved just as this young one was doing, taking measurements, spreading out bales of cloth, and consulting the fashion papers. Lady Maisie sighed as she remembered those joyful times.

'Mum,' said Rowan, not very sure where her sudden idea had come from, 'perhaps you ought to go for some sort of more old-fashioned look.'

Petronella, who was poring over the latest *Bridal Wear* with Chantal the dressmaker, raised her head. 'What exactly do you mean, darling?'

'I was just remembering,' said Rowan slowly, 'you know how you want to wear tartan, well, there's a portrait of Lady Maisie McNeil in one of Robert's old books, and she's wearing the most beautiful tartan dress with a sort of lace collar and a long full skirt.'

'I see,' said Petronella, a wonderful smile lighting her face, 'I could be dressed for my wedding just like the heroine of Robert's most famous book!'

'Yes, and you could do your hair just the same. Lady Maisie's is all held up with little combs and things.'

In fact, the only difference between her pretty mother and the Scottish belle would be that Petronella was very pregnant.

'That's an absolutely inspired idea! And we won't tell Robert, it'll be our little secret until the great day. Bryony, isn't your little sister a genius?'

Bryony, who was sitting in a corner, reading a book on Celtic design which she had brought with her, said nothing.

Lady Maisie, however, found herself

strangely touched by the bairn's suggestion. Mistress Petronella was as great a fool as she'd met in her many hauntings, but she had a bonnie face, and despite her great belly, would not look amiss in the ghost's clothing. And she was pleased that Rowan had allowed the phantom memory to steal into her head.

'So what style exactly are we speaking about?' Chantal, a trim young woman in black shirt and trousers, had produced a sketch pad and pencil.

'Mid-eighteenth century, I suppose,' said Petronella.

'Yes, just like that,' said Rowan, admiring Chantal's swift drawing. 'A very low neck and a tight bodice.'

'Yes,' said the designer, 'I can see that working. We'd have to raise the waistline obviously—' and three heads, Chantal's blond bob, Petronella's coiled plaits, and Rowan's light brown curls, bent eagerly over the sketch. Only Bryony remained unimpressed.

Lady Maisie, herself, was in quite a flutter at seeing her favourite gown flow from the young woman's clever fingers, but she dared not tarry whilst McCantrip might be up to mischief. His attic was but a ghostly hop from the dressmaker's building, so in half a second, Lady Maisie was by Will's side, watching as he did up his jerkin with the amazing little metal teeth which so took her fancy. If only such a contraption had been at hand in her time! How many hours would've been saved from the pernickety business of lacing, pinning and knotting. Here was McCantrip, ready for the day in less time than it took to fry a collop!

Lady Maisie followed the young man down the staircase, where he was greeted by one of the men who were restoring the apartments.

'Hey, Will, still ahead o' the landlord, eh? It would be a shame if anyone telt on you, so it would. You up for a bevvy the night, by the way?'

So McCantrip was lavishing ale upon the workmen so that they would not tell the owner of the building that he was living there illegally! Just the sort of mean-spirited trick the ghost would've suspected.

She followed him out into the Cowgate, up and down a vennel or two, and into a coffee house. There, to her surprise, Lady Maisie saw two rows of the selfsame printing devices which Monteith and the bairns had in their chambers. Before each machine, seemingly entranced by the uncanny light it shed, sat a young mortal.

McCantrip sat down at one of the beasts, and Lady Maisie was behind him in an instant. She had seen Monteith at work in the past, and watched eagerly to see what words McCantrip would cast onto the screen.

It was a letter.

'Dear Sis,

Hot on the trail! I sweet-talked Rowan's mom into inviting me back to the old homestead for supper next week. I know a week's a long time to wait, but it's safer than sneaking in and getting caught again. So you just hold on, and believe I'll make the most of the opportunity when it comes. The mom – Petronella – has never been to Alaska, but I reckon I can solve that puzzle when the time comes. So you just order yourself up that tartan heritage gown and prepare to trash Alvin McCantrip

**and all his kin at the next Virginia
Gathering**
   Wish me luck
      Will'

And before Lady Maisie could make head
or tail of the mysterious words, the entire
message quivered and vanished as a marsh
sprite would dissolve at the first blink of the
rising sun. In its place, the ghost read
'MESSAGE DELIVERED'.

Message delivered where? It was one of
those moments when Lady Maisie could've
torn her pretty hair in frustration. It used
to take several days, if not weeks, for a
messenger to carry a letter up glens and over
mountains – so where had McCantrip's words
so strangely sped?

SIX

A week had now passed since the reading and the first visit to the dressmaker, and once again Rowan woke up feeling restless and ill at ease. She sat up in bed and looked at the rocking chair. Could it possibly be moving very, very slightly? For some reason, first thing every morning, she had the sensation that someone was sitting there, watching her.

Ridiculous. She jumped out of bed and padded across the room to open the curtains. At least she knew why she was bad-tempered today. Will McCantrip was coming to supper. He had been mentioned only once since Mum had issued the invitation, and that was when Robert had reported that he'd been unable to admit him to his economics course. Will had not only applied too late, but he didn't have the qualifications. Or rather, his qualifications hadn't arrived.

'Says they've been lost in the post,' Robert had said. 'Perfectly possible. The US mail isn't nearly as efficient as ours.'

'But surely you could make allowances if they've been lost?' Petronella, eating supper, had paused before taking a dainty nibble of pasta.

'No, no, we have to go by the rules. If we let in any Tom, Dick or Harriet who turned up without qualifications, the place would be a perfect bear garden.'

Rowan had had a vision of Mr Bear and his friends taking over the university, munching honey sandwiches during lectures, and falling asleep in the library.

'It's no laughing matter, Rowan! I'm sorry, Petronella, I know Will's keen, but I can't make an exception for him.'

'But he's come all this way just to study with you, darling!'

Robert had smiled complacently. 'I must

admit I'm flattered, but rules are rules.'

And that had seemed to be the end of the matter, but Rowan, try as she might, couldn't get the young man out of her head. At home, at school, during all the wedding preparations, she seemed to feel his piercing eyes following her.

And tonight she really would see him again.

'Aye, lassie, and who knows to what ends?' Lady Maisie, reclining in the rocking chair, shook her head. She still found it easy to read Rowan's thoughtwaves, but the patterns of other mortals were becoming confused to her, a sure sign of her waning powers. What if she should slip into nothingness before she could discover McCantrip's fell purpose?

Never! The valiant phantom refused to entertain the idea for an instant. A McNeil had never yet failed a friend, and at not matter what cost, Lady Maisie would uphold the honour of her clan.

Borne aloft by her brave thoughts, Lady Maisie floated behind Rowan as the child descended once more to the family kitchen. The aristocratic ghost was shocked that Monteith and his brood should be forced to eat there, and as she took her accustomed place on the dresser, her little feet tucked between the plates, Lady Maisie lamented yet again the lofty halls of Clachanfeckle. She could not have lived thus, slopping backwards and forwards between table and press, preparing her own miserable little meal as the lassies were doing. At least their mother had a decent repast, a great dish of eggs with flakes of smoked salmon stirred into them.

'I'm just so hungry these days, morning, noon and night – but particularly morning!' Petronella laughed apologetically as she forked up the delicacy.

'And quite right too, darling. You simply have to look after *both* of yourselves.' That was the doltish Monteith, looking lovingly at his mistress.

Lady Maisie shuddered with disgust.

'You are remembering that Will's coming to supper tonight, sweetheart?'

'Of course. To make up to him for his disappointment about my class, I'm going to cook him a traditional Scottish meal.'

'Fish and chips?'

'Certainly not, Bryony! Roast pheasant

with rowan jelly and claret sauce and curly kale, and a sherry trifle for pudding.'

'What if he's a vegetarian like me?'

'Well, Bryony, as I was planning to make a pasta dish for you, Will can share that if he also shares your ideals.'

'It won't be specially Scottish, though.' That was Rowan.

'I can't make allowances for everyone's fads and fancies—'

Monteith, to Lady Maisie's pleasure, was going red. He dipped his twisted bannock into his coffee and bit off the sopping end. 'Whatever you make will be delicious. As always.'

Petronella continued soothingly. 'And girls, tomorrow morning, first thing, the dressmaker's for a second fitting.'

Lady Maisie could see an actual black cloud gathering in the air above the bairns' heads, and if their mother couldn't see it, she quite possibly sensed its presence, for she turned briskly to her sweetheart.

'And your kilt, Robert, you have organized it, haven't you? You simply can't leave hiring it until the last moment. And if you look as splendid in it as I expect, perhaps you could have one actually made for future formal occasions.'

'I'm hardly going to be getting married again.'

'But there will be *other* opportunities. Christenings, for example.' Petronella looked modestly downwards and, once again, the ghost shuddered. Squawling infants had never been of the least interest to her. 'It's such a pity there isn't a Monteith tartan. You ought to be wearing your own tartan at your wedding.'

'There is a McCantrip of Monteith. Quite pretty. Dark blue and green.'

'McCantrip – that's Will's name! Do you think there might be some family connection?'

Rowan's hand, halfway to her mouth, shook so hard that she almost dropped her toast. Will McCantrip a relation?

Robert, however, laughed. 'I doubt it. These old links are worn pretty thin nowadays.'

Aye, and a sorry state of affairs that was, thought Lady Maisie, soaring in disgust through the window and out over the garden. Why, when she was a lass— In the very act of clearing the hedge, the ghost paused. Below her crouched the faithful white hound, his eyes fixed on the kitchen door. Lady Maisie had seen him wait for Rowan before, and was impressed. He might be a small beast, but he was obviously as true-hearted as had been her great deerhounds, Gordon and Gruach.

Then the ghost observed something. The dog was sitting upright, ears pricked, the hairs rising on his neck and throat.

He knew that she was there.

Lady Maisie's dead heart bounded. Atholl, so much more sensitive than any porridge-headed mortal, could feel her presence! In fact, he was both growling and wagging his tail, in obvious confusion.

'Intelligent beastie,' said Lady Maisie, descending to run her hand over Atholl's quivering fur. 'If only thon Rowan shared your abilities.'

Rowan was splashing towards them down the wet path, on her way to school.

'What's wrong, Atholl? Seen a cat, have you?'

Lady Maisie chuckled silently.

'It's Saturday tomorrow, I've got to go to the manky old dressmaker's in the morning, but after lunch I'll take you out for a proper run, OK?'

For once, Atholl didn't try to jump up on her school skirt with his muddy paws. Instead, he ran round in circles, snapping at thin air.

'So don't show your gratitude.'

The ghost, a little ashamed of herself for teasing a dumb beast, floated to the top of the hedge.

'That's more like my favourite Scottie dog,' said Rowan, as Atholl rubbed himself against her, and Lady Maisie, remembering how her own great hounds would lay their heads in her silken lap, felt the suspicion of a tear in her eye.

But this was no behaviour for a McNeil! She was indeed growing old. Pulling herself together, the ghost whisked upwards and surfed towards the Old Town on the back of an easterly wind.

A little light haunting would soon raise her spirits.

SEVEN

Rowan pushed open the garden gate and went cautiously up the path. Ever since she'd come home and found Will sprawled in the kitchen, she had felt uneasy upon entering the garden. Once again, the light was on, and she peeped in the window, keeping well back behind the dripping rosebushes.

Robert was standing at the table, whipping up a huge bowl of cream. He was wearing what Rowan thought of as his show-off cooking clothes: linen slacks, an open-necked shirt, and a chef's apron.

As she let herself in, Rowan thought that this was probably the first time she'd actually been glad to see Robert, but she didn't allow herself to look pleased.

'Hello, Robert,' she said. 'Where's Mum?'

'She went to see some florist with Mollie. I'm not even thinking about it.'

Several pans were boiling or simmering on the hob, and there was a delicious old-fashioned smell of roasting meat.

'So is this the famous Scottish dinner?'

'It certainly is,' said Robert. 'Non-vegetarian and very fattening. Everything is organic, though. Oh, except Bryony's pasta.'

Rowan almost laughed along with him, but stopped herself just in time.

'And I'm making my mother's old-fashioned sherry trifle for pudding. It's almost like your favourite tiramisu.'

This time Rowan absolutely had to smile. 'Oh yum,' she said. 'Thank you, Robert.'

Robert did have his uses. Mum never made puddings because of watching her weight, but Robert's were absolutely gorgeous: double-chocolate mousse, brown bread ice-cream, bramble upside-down cake.

Licking her lips at the thought of tonight's treat, Rowan turned to go, just as the front doorbell rang.

'I'll get that,' she said.

'No, no, I'll do it.' Robert hustled past her. 'I'm expecting a delivery. You, er, check nothing's boiling over.'

Rowan stepped back into the kitchen, but watched as Robert accepted two packages, one square, one long and thin, thanked the messenger, and shut the front door.

'Not a word to your mother,' he whispered to Rowan as, with exaggerated care, he carried the mysterious parcels up to his study. Honestly, Mum's sense of drama must be catching. Surely Robert never used to behave like that?

Rowan went up to her own room to change for dinner. She didn't always bother, but she wanted to show Will McCantrip that she wasn't some little schoolgirl he could boss around. Accordingly, she took off her uniform and wriggled into jeans and her favourite leafy green T-shirt. Then she looked at herself in the mirror as she brushed her hair and tucked it back into a clip. What would the medallion look like against the green material? There would be no harm in trying it on for just a second. Mum wasn't even in the house.

Rowan removed the little package from her box, unwrapped the fishy-smelling leather, and dropped the chain over her head. As she'd suspected it would, the medallion gleamed, the enamel on the tiny leaves reflecting the green of her shirt. Alice's present really would add the final touch to Mum's wedding outfit.

That wretched wedding again! Lady Maisie, tired out after a long and fruitless day of haunting Will, had been asleep in the rocking chair until Rowan's thoughts awoke her. Since her return to Dryburgh Place she had heard enough about Mistress Petronella's wedding to last her for several lifetimes. So the lassies were giving this bauble to their mother? It was dainty enough, but a trifle old-fashioned to the ghost's eye. She would've preferred a fine rope of pearls.

'Robert, we're both here! I met Will coming up the path. What a wonderful smell, what *have* you made for us? Will, just leave your jacket in the hall.'

Both Rowan and the ghost jumped. They

had been so intent on examining the golden trinket that neither had heard Petronella and Will entering the hall. Rowan snatched off the medallion and dropped it hastily into her jewellery box. Then she shoved the box back amongst the huddle of CDs, dusty hairclips, books and make-up on her dressing-table and ran silently from the room.

Lady Maisie regarded the mess with a nostalgic smile. What a slattern the lassie was, not unlike the ghost herself in her own youth. When the jewel casket had failed to close she hadn't even tarried to fasten it, just as Lady Maisie herself had once flung down her horsewhip and gloves and the diamond earrings which she had worn when his Royal Highness Prince Charles Edward Stuart had honoured them with his presence – but this was no time to dwell on the past!

If McCantrip's purpose was to be discovered, there was some serious haunting to be done.

Rowan, meanwhile, had crept along the landing and was peering over the banister. Petronella, who couldn't enter a room without a certain amount of rush and flurry, was making a big production of ushering her new friend into the family home. Her pregnant figure looked odder than ever from above, like one of these bulging loaves of foreign bread in the deli, but she was whisking about as nimbly as ever, first into the kitchen to greet Robert, and then back into the hall to gush around Will.

'Robert, beloved, you haven't actually *roasted* something for us? Will, come this way, make yourself at home, can I offer you a glass of wine?'

Without his cap and jacket, the young man looked more of a nerd than ever. His skinny body was clad in jeans and a plaid shirt, and his ponytail trailed down his shoulders. What he really needed, in Rowan's opinion, wasn't a glass of Robert's carefully chosen wine, but a good washing and brushing.

As Will followed Mum into the kitchen, Rowan went silently downstairs, straight to his jacket, and dug into the pockets.

'So this is how we welcome the weary traveller to oor wee hielan' hame?'

Rowan almost leapt out of her trainers. Bryony had come in and was looking at her curiously.

'What on earth are you doing?'

'Ssshhh!' Rowan waved her hands frantically. 'Will's in the kitchen. I'm looking for clues.'

'Such as?'

'I don't know. Anything. Anything to prove he's got some dark reason for being here.'

'Dark reason! You've been watching too much *Buffy*.'

'Look at this!' Rowan held up a slim leather folder. 'It's his driving licence.'

'So?'

'He might've given us a false name . . . oh.' Rowan's voice dropped.

'Has he?'

'No.'

Will's full name was William Patrick Charles McCantrip and he lived at Mavis Creek, Callender, Virginia.

'That just proves he's telling the truth about his family being Scottish. There's a place called Callender in Scotland. His ancestors probably came from near there.'

'Perhaps.' Rowan wasn't ready to agree with her sister. 'But it might be a fake.'

'Tattie-head. Put it back before Mum comes looking for us.'

'But there's more stuff here, photos—'

Rowan stopped short as she looked at the brightly-coloured snapshot. It showed a young teenage girl, with Will's red hair and beaky nose, posed on a sunny verandah. She was sitting in a wheelchair.

'What is it?' Bryony looked over her shoulder.

'She must be Will's sister. Or something.'

The girl was looking up with the bad-tempered expression of someone taken by surprise.

'Put it away,' said Bryony. 'We shouldn't be looking at his stuff.'

Rowan, feeling as though her fingers were sticky with guilt, shoved everything back into the wallet, just as Mum's voice came trilling from the kitchen.

'Darlings, is that you? Come along!'

Rowan hurriedly replaced the wallet in Will's jacket and followed Bryony into the room.

'Just in time! Say hello to Will.' Petronella, a ridiculously small frilly apron tied around the remains of her waist, was putting out cutlery and napkins, watched by Will, who was already seated, wineglass in hand.

The girls nodded in Will's direction, and

Rowan was certain that the look he gave her through his smeary spectacles was cunning and foxy. Just what was he sniffing after in their home?

'Petronella, you sit down at once and let the girls do the heavy work,' commanded Robert, as he drained the kale.

'You can hardly call a napkin *heavy*!' cried Petronella, sinking nonetheless into her chair.

'But you've been running around with Mollie all afternoon, haven't you?'

And what do you think I've been doing? grouched Rowan to herself as she finished laying the table. Double French *and* Maths *and* History.

'I wasn't running around, Robert. Mollie was driving, and we only went to the florist's. I've ordered my bouquet – white roses, so Scottish, the Jacobite flower, you know. I thought it would be a nice compliment to your clan, darling. And posies for you girls.'

Petronella's words had a strong effect upon her audience. Robert smiled, obviously pleased by this romantic notion, Rowan and Bryony looked disgusted, and Lady Maisie, seated once more upon the dresser, found herself touching the white rose upon her own breast.

'Charles Edward! My bonnie Prince!' she murmured.

Even Will seemed impressed. 'So your family were supporters of the royal Stuarts, Dr Monteith?'

'Not just supporters, actually connected,' said Petronella proudly.

'No, no.' Robert waved his hand modestly. 'Very distantly. Long ago.'

'That sure must be something.' Will's eyes were definitely gleaming. 'You know, where I come from, our Scottish heritage sure is important to us.'

'And that reminds me, Will—' Petronella's face was alight with excitement. '– did you know that the McCantrips and the Monteiths are actually related?'

Why did Will suddenly look uncomfortable?

'Um, yeah,' he said, 'I did once hear something like that. In fact, my grandaddy—'

'Now, Petronella, do stop quizzing Will about all these old stories. I'm sure he wants his supper as much as I do.' Robert piled dishes of tasty-looking food upon the table. 'I know that I never think about my noble ancestors.'

'I'm not eating these dead birds.' Bryony was looking scornfully at Robert's banquet.

'And for your pleasure, ma'am'selle!' Robert produced a bowl of pasta in green basil sauce and put it at Bryony's place.

Defeated, she sat down, muttering her thanks.

'Some pheasant, Will? You're not another veggie, I trust?'

'No, sir, I certainly am not, although I, like, respect the rights of those who are.' And he made a smarmy little bow in Bryony's direction.

Rowan shivered as she looked at him. Why was he trying so hard to charm her family? And why was no-one else suspicious of him?

Aye, why indeed? wondered Lady Maisie. It was as clear as moonlight to the ghost that McCantrip was up to some mischief, yet only yon Rowan had the psychic ability to be aware of it. The rest of her family were as sensitive as platters of haggis.

'Roast potatoes, Will? Not entirely authentic, I'm afraid.' Robert was serving the food, beaming with pride as guest and family murmured their appreciation.

Taking her first mouthful, Rowan had

to admit that the meal was delicious.

'Darling, you've surpassed yourself!' cried Petronella. 'If whatever you prepare for the reception is half as good as this, our guests will be absolutely bowled over!' She turned to Will. 'You must forgive me babbling on like this about our wedding, but it is totally all I can think about. Of course, we would've got married long ago, but there have been endless delays. Robert's ex-wife is a great traveller, Mongolia, Siberia, Alaska—'

'The first Mrs Monteith has been in Alaska recently?'

Why did Will pick up so swiftly on Mum's words?

'Why, yes, quite recently, I think.' Petronella was taken aback. 'When did that parcel come, Bryony?'

'The beginning of last week.'

Everyone was looking at Will. He laughed awkwardly. 'I have relatives in Alaska, so I'm always interested to hear about the place. And so this Mrs Monteith actually sent you a souvenir? A T-shirt or something?'

'No, she sent me this great nose-ring. And a wee carving for Rowan.'

'It sure was generous of her to send you

presents.' Will glanced rapidly from one sister to the other as he said this. 'You must've been surprised.'

'Nothing would surprise us about Alice,' said Petronella swiftly, looking at Robert. Alice was a forbidden subject in the household.

Will took the hint. 'So you're planning a real traditional wedding, Petronella?'

'We certainly are! A friend is lending us her beautiful old house down by the Water of Leith and we're having the actual ceremony in the garden. I'll be wearing the loveliest dress – now, you know I can't describe it, Robert, it has to be kept a secret from the groom! – and Robert is going to wear the kilt, aren't you, Robert?' Petronella glanced merrily at her husband-to-be.

'Yes, Robert, you'll really have to wear a kilt,' said Rowan.

'I'm considering it,' he said airily, and Rowan almost thought that he winked at her.

'We're all ganging up on you,' said Petronella.

'I sure would've expected you to wear Highland dress, sir,' put in Will.

'You see, even Will agrees with us.'

'Why,' the young man continued, 'even I've got a kilt back home, to wear when I'm piping.'

'Will!' Petronella dropped her knife and fork. 'You don't mean to say you actually play the pipes?'

A smile lit Will's face as he said humbly, 'Only for the past few years. My dad taught me. Of course, I'm nothing like as good as the guys you have over here.'

'But a piper is exactly what we need! I simply can't believe it! Fate has led you to us – now we can have a piper at the wedding.'

Robert, seeing the tiny wedding getting even bigger, looked alarmed. He took a soothing gulp of red wine. 'But, my dear, we can't expect Will to fall in with our plans—'

'No, no, no, we can't have a proper Scottish wedding without a piper, and I'm sure you'll play for us, won't you, Will?'

'Petronella, Dr Monteith, I'd be just honoured.'

Rowan looked at Will. He was absolutely smirking with pleasure, and yes, triumph. He had got his own way. He had squirmed right into the heart of the family.

Lady Maisie, as alarmed as Rowan, was also watching as Will, eating and drinking like the veriest glutton, declared that he would search out the best of tunes for the wedding and how fortunate it was that he had brought his pipes with him.

'Marie-Rose, that's my sister, said I couldn't come to Scotland without my pipes, and was she right!'

So Marie-Rose must be the person to whom he had sent the mysterious flying letter.

'I'm going to start practising the minute I get home. I sure won't let you down, Petronella.' Will was getting up now and heading for the door. He hesitated. 'Uh – where's the—? I think I'll just—'

'First door to the right, top of the stairs,' said Petronella.

'Thanks.' Will climbed the stairs, Lady Maisie behind him. How ridiculously modest mortals were nowadays, she thought, and as for that noisy, newfangled flushing device, what was wrong with the tried and trusty chamberpot?

At the head of the stairs, however, Will hesitated by Rowan's half-open door, but only for an instant. He took a torch from his pocket, and giving off waves of fear, excitement and desire, quickly swept the beam around the room. Then he stepped inside, closed the door, and with one leap was beside the dressing-table and rummaging through Rowan's treasures. The light had caught the gold links of the chain as they spilled from the jewel box, and Will had only to fling back the tiny lid, and the medallion itself was clasped in his sweaty hand!

His face ablaze with triumph and delight, Will stuffed the medallion in his pocket, sped from Rowan's room to the water-closet, and then paused for a moment to admire himself in the looking glass.

'William McCantrip,' he murmured, 'you are the coolest, cleverest, wickedess dude! Go, McCantrip, go, go!'

Lady Maisie, completely beside herself, battered Will's foxy head with her fists. He had supped with the family and then stolen the lassies' wedding gift! If only she could slice at him with her claymore!

Will, however, was simply puzzled by the sudden draught.

'Kinda chilly, these old houses,' was the thought that, to her despair, the ghost picked up.

'If this had been two hundred and fifty years ago, you creepie-crawlie callant, it's more than a chill you would be feeling! It would be cold steel!'

And Lady Maisie hurled herself through the floorboards to the kitchen, where Rowan was clearing the table. She spun about the lassie, trying, with every shred of her failing strength to convey a warning. In a moment, McCantrip would be marching out of the house, the golden gift safely in his pocket.

The lass stopped, and put a hand to the back of her neck. Then she went to the window, drew back the curtain, and peered out.

'No, no!' raged Lady Maisie. 'The other way, you daft hizzie!'

In the hall, Monteith and Petronella were bidding their guest farewell.

'Rowan, come and say goodnight to Will.'

The child obeyed her mother's command.

'Turn out his pockets!' screamed Lady Maisie, but although she was throwing out as much energy as a roomful of candles, no-one heard her.

Rowan did, indeed, look suspiciously at

Will's beaming face, but he was already half-way over the threshold.

'Give me your mobile number, Will, and I'll phone you when I have a kilt sorted out for you. Mollie's son's about your size.'

Will gave his number. 'Sure thing, Petronella, I'll look forward to it. And thanks again for the great meal.'

And then he was gone, down the dark garden with two eager bounds.

Lady Maisie howled with frustration. Then two things occurred to her. Now that he had stolen Mistress Petronella's golden gift, surely he would not have the brass neck to play at her wedding?

And it was more than simple poverty which had led him to theft. It was the medallion itself which he had wanted.

'He will be clean away in a second, lassie!' she exclaimed. 'Raise the alarm before it is too late!'

And once more she threw herself at Rowan – but to no avail. Lady Maisie, however, had been a military leader in her day, and if one tactic failed, she was ready to try another. Giving Rowan's shoulders one final, icy shake, she then sped through the window and over the hedge into the next-door garden.

Rowan wondered why she felt so cold. Because the front door had been open whilst Will said his goodbyes, she supposed. But this was a more deadly chill which made her shiver as though a cold hand were stroking the back of her neck.

And how odd Will had looked! If she were cold, he seemed to be positively burning. Of course, he'd had several glasses of wine which would account for his flushed cheeks, yet there was more to it than that. He'd reminded Rowan of an athlete standing on the gold medal step after some great sporting triumph. If he hadn't been saying polite goodbyes, he could well have been punching his fist in the air.

So why was he so happy? When he'd gone upstairs, he'd just seemed quietly pleased with himself – and five minutes later he'd come down as though he'd won the World Cup.

The cold hand which had been ruffling her hair grasped Rowan by the throat. That first evening when she'd come home and suspected that Will was a thief— Rowan shot up the stairs.

Her door was wide open – had she left

it like that? But what did she have worth stealing?

Only one thing.

Already knowing what she would find, Rowan leapt across the floor to her dressing-table. Yes, there lay her jewellery box, all her little clips and bangles safe and sound – but no medallion.

For one awful moment the freezing chill closed around her heart. Mum's wonderful present was gone. And how could she confess her carelessness to Bryony? She hadn't locked the box.

But then a wave of energy surged through her. Would she let Will get away with the theft? No chance! Rowan raced down the stairs, snatched her jacket from its peg, and let herself quietly out into the night.

EIGHT

Which way would he have gone? If Will hoped to attend the university he'd probably be living near the centre of town, so Rowan turned left and set off at a gallop. It was a scary night for a chase. Clouds raced across the sky, and there was a mysterious scuffling and rustling in the fallen leaves, almost as though she were being followed.

And there was Will, just ahead of her. She'd guessed correctly!

For the next couple of blocks, Rowan followed cautiously. Will had only to glance back and he'd see her in the otherwise empty street. Then he reached the main road and she was able to close the gap between them by lurking behind a big group of students. At the foot of the road, however, as Rowan well knew, lay the Meadows.

By day, the Meadows was simply a stretch of open grass crossed by tree-lined paths, but at night the occasional lamps cast terrifying shadows and the footsteps of those bold enough to walk there were swiftly muffled by an eerie silence.

Will plunged down Jawbone Walk, so named because the giant jawbone of a whale formed a grisly entrance to the path and trotted off under the trees, moving in his characteristic scurry, head down, shoulders hunched.

Rowan followed. She dodged from tree to tree, too intent on her prey to be frightened – although it did seem to her that the scuffling sounds which she had barely noticed in Dryburgh Place were even louder and scarier out here in the open.

But creepy though crossing the park might be, it was actually the easy bit. Once Will reached the far side, she'd be in danger of losing him in the lanes and closes of the Old

Town. Rowan speeded up, and just behind her hastened the ghost herself, curls, plaid and petticoat streaming out behind her.

'Och, but I cannot be moving at this pace much longer!' wailed Lady Maisie. 'And all this kerfuffle over a fairing!'

She stayed at Rowan's shoulder all along the High Street and then to the depths of the Cowgate. Having already seen Will's hide-out, she feared that the lassie might be walking into a very nasty trap.

And indeed, it was only now as Rowan found herself creeping down a particularly narrow vennel that she began to be afraid.

Apart from Will and herself, the wynd was completely empty, so if he looked back, she'd be lost. Rowan kept close to the wall, ready to duck into a doorway should he turn round.

On and on Will went whilst Rowan followed, freezing, shaking, but absolutely determined not to give up the chase. She had no idea where her courage came from but she simply would not let Mum's present vanish along with Will into the night.

Then he slipped round a final corner, halted before a gloomy, disused building and drew something from his pocket. Rowan caught the tiny flash of metal and darted forward to crouch in the next doorway. Her mind seemed to be working independently of her shivering body because, at the sight of the keys, she realized that if the door which Will was about to unlock was fixed to a self-closing device as tenement doors usually were, it would swing slowly shut behind him – so slowly, perhaps, that she might be able to creep in before the catch snapped home. She balanced on her toes, ready to sprint towards the entrance the moment Will disappeared. Will, contrarily, had slowed down. He was sorting through his ring of keys, holding them up to the faint glow of a distant streetlamp. Then, just when Rowan could bear the tension no longer, he fitted one of the keys into the lock, pushed open the door and vanished inside.

Rowan bounded forward, covered the cracked paving stones at one leap and threw herself against the door exactly as the tongue of the lock grated against the socket. She was just in time to prevent it from clicking home and very, very cautiously she eased the door open and slipped inside – only to find, to her horror, that the stairway inside was totally dark.

Or at least she assumed it must be a stairway. For all she knew, she might be facing some huge empty space with Will lurking in some corner of it, or the whole floor might have fallen in, leaving nothing ahead of her but a few floorboards balanced over gaping cellars. One wrong step and she would tumble into the darkness. And no-one knew where she was! If, for whatever unthinkable reason, she never returned home, her family would have no idea where to look for her. Yet despite the gruesome thoughts racketing through her head, Rowan snibbed the lock open so that she could make a quick getaway, and then, a step at a time, she inched forward, keeping one hand pressed against the clammy wall and the other stretched out in front of her.

Then, at last, she felt rather than saw a larger, airier space around her and realized that she must have emerged from a passage into the actual stairwell. And yes, a tiny glimmer of light was circling above her, spiralling and receding. Will must be climbing the stairs with a torch. If he could climb, at least the staircase must be sound, so Rowan mounted after him, still keeping close to the wall and feeling her way at each step.

Lady Maisie, meanwhile, beside herself with anxiety, flitted between pursuer and pursued, cursing her inability to either help Rowan or hinder Will.

'Ochone, ochone, that I should have survived, alive or dead, to see this shameful day!' And wringing her hands, the ghost soared through the darkness, howling with despair.

Her howls, naturally, were inaudible to the human ear, but somewhere nearby a different pair of ears pricked up and a jawful of teeth, as white as Will's own, slavered and snapped.

Rowan climbed steadfastly on. What she would do when Will eventually came to a halt, she had no idea. It was enough that she had tracked him to his lair. If need be, she could come back the next day, she could fetch the police, she could— The light disappeared. Rowan had been staring at it so hard that she blinked and stumbled, landing sprawled across the stone staircase.

Above her came the faint click of a door

closing. Will McCantrip had reached home.

Rowan picked herself up and scuttled up the final steps, paying less heed to moving quietly than to fixing the point of Will's disappearance. Yes, here was the door. Rowan ran her fingers up and down it and, finding a large, old-fashioned keyhole, bent down and peeped in.

Darkness. Then a flicker of light, and a faint but steady glow. Will had lit a candle, and to Rowan's relief, he stood in the centre of her limited field of vision, staring intently down at the small object which he held in his hand. The medallion! And only a few feet away from her, on the other side of the solid door. She had to get it back.

'A lassie after my own heart!' cried Lady Maisie, who was whisking backwards and forwards through the door, not at all put out by its solidity. When she was Rowan's age, she'd been equally fearless. Had she not slain the Black Hound of Breadalbane and dared the terrible kelpie who guarded the Falls of Cragganmore?

Rowan, keeping her eye glued to the keyhole, saw Will put the medallion down, very gently, on the table, before stepping out of sight. Had he actually left the room? Just above the keyhole there was the slim handle of a more modern lock and Rowan, heart thudding in her throat, pressed it down and pushed.

The door gave at the pressure. Will, drunk with wine and triumph, had forgotten to lock it! Rowan opened the door a little further, and scarcely breathing, edged herself into the room. When there was no yell of surprise, no rustle of Will leaping forward to grab her, Rowan took another step. The medallion lay only a metre or so away from her, gleaming in the pool of candlelight.

Where was Will? At the far end of the room there was a curtained recess, and from behind it, Rowan could hear water running and a kettle being filled. Without hesitating to think, she pounced, snatched the medallion, and fled.

Running down the stairs in the pitch dark was the most terrifying thing that Rowan had ever done. One hand clutching the medallion, the other fumbling for the banister, she stumbled and fell and ran again, whilst a distant, disbelieving part of her brain refused to accept her danger.

Then there was a roar – no, an absolute scream of fury, loss and despair behind her, and immediately the beam of Will's torch flickered over the walls of the stairwell, backwards and forwards, up and down, until it settled and held upon her fleeing form. Rowan was now running for her life, down stairs, along landings, turn and descend, turn again and descend, whilst Will, advantaged by his longer legs, leapt after her, gaining ground at every step.

Rowan, now halfway down the interminable stairs, swung herself round a newel post and saw, barely a metre ahead of her, something impossible.

Something which stood between her and the outer door. Something which crouched and snarled and whose yellow eyes and white teeth glistened horribly in the approaching light of Will's torch.

NINE

Rowan had not thought it possible to be any more frightened than she already was, but seeing the creature before her, she felt as though she might actually faint with terror. The animal appeared to be on its haunches, ready to spring, and Rowan had no doubt as to where it planned to sink its teeth.

It would almost be better to fall into Will's clutches than be savaged by this fearsome beast, so she tried to make herself move backwards, away from the animal – if animal it was. But Rowan couldn't move. She stood frozen against the banister, her entire body locked tight, and only distantly aware that behind her Will had also halted.

The beast growled, the thick white fur on its throat framing the terrible teeth and glittering eyes. Then it tensed and leapt, its body a blur of thistledown as, barely displacing the air, it sailed past Rowan's knee.

Past her *knee*? The tiny, soft-coated creature which was darting up the stairs and straight for Will's ankles was suddenly wonderfully familiar.

Atholl! Loyal, noble Atholl must have followed her all the way from Dryburgh Place!

Rowan, who had only a second ago been rigid with fright, almost sank down onto the stairs in her relief. She had not imagined the mysterious noises behind her. Atholl had been hot on her trail every pawstep of the way.

'Och the valiant wee hound!' Lady Maisie was equally relieved and delighted. Her plan had succeeded! When she had failed to warn Rowan about Will's thieving, she had sped next door and roused Atholl from his fireside slumber. It had been easy to make him persuade his mistress to let him out and, once alert to Rowan's danger, he had taken off after her as fast as his short little legs would carry him. Now the ghost spun up the centre of the stairwell, whooping triumphantly.

'On, on, my brave beastie! Sink your teeth into his miserable shins, gnaw his shanks to mincemeat! Och but you are a bonnie fighter!'

Rowan got back to her feet and, holding tightly to the banister, ran down the remaining flight of stairs. As her feet touched level ground, the beam of Will's torch, which had been swinging wildly over walls and ceiling as he fended off Atholl's attack, snapped out and he yowled with pain. Atholl's sharp little teeth had sunk home!

Rowan, feeling in the dark for the passage wall, took the few remaining steps to the door, fumbled for the catch and, as her fingers closed around it, called back up the stairs for Atholl.

'Come on, boy, leave him!'

But to her dismay there was no answering patter of little paws. From the yelps and growls which mingled with Will's cries, it was obvious that the dog was enjoying himself too much to obey her. Rowan attempted to whistle but no sound came from her dry lips.

'Atholl, *drop it*, boy! Drop it!' she shouted

in as commanding a tone as possible and Atholl, as though he were spitting out something nasty dredged from the bottom of a river, let go of Will's unsavoury leg and bounded down the stairs to her side.

'Oh *Atholl*!' Tears of gratitude running down her face, Rowan scooped up the heroic little dog, opened the door and fled down the moonlit wynd. If Will were still following her, his injuries must have been slowing him down because there was no sound of pursuit. Nonetheless, Rowan ran for all she was worth, surprised that she could still move at all, surprised that she could still think sufficiently clearly to recognize her surroundings and plan the swiftest route home.

Lady Maisie, having seen Rowan and Atholl safely on their way, swooped back to check on Will. The young man, to her disgust, was shivering in his room, dabbing at his bleeding ankle with the least grubby corner of a large grey towel.

'The miserable coward!' hissed the ghost. 'To allow one wee hound to rob him of his prize!'

Almost visible sparks of scorn flashed from her lovely hazel eyes and Will shuddered and glanced uneasily over his shoulder. For a wonderful moment, Lady Maisie thought that Will could feel her awful presence, but alas, from the manner in which his gaze fastened itself upon the door, it was obvious that he was really afraid that Atholl might be lurking outside.

It was a new experience for the ghost to be considered as less terrifying than a very small dog and it infuriated her.

'New World poltroon! McCantrip though you might be, take warning! You have aroused the wrath of Lady Maisie McNeil. There will be no mercy.'

And leaving Will crouched miserably in his squalid room, the ghost floated out in search of Rowan and Atholl. Normally, she had no trouble in locking onto the thought-waves of whoever she planned to haunt but she had noticed, since her latest return to Edinburgh, that this ability appeared to be diminishing. And tonight, as she attempted to find Rowan in the maze of narrow streets below her, Lady Maisie found herself hastening backwards and forwards over roofs and gables like any novice. Almost panicking, she sorted through the incomprehensible thoughtwaves cluttering up the airspace – 'Shall we go for an Indian or a pizza?' 'Who do you fancy for the big game?' – until she picked up Rowan's signal, a plaintive longing to be safe at home in bed. Lady Maisie, being a ghost, had few tender feelings but something like pity welled up in her heart. Poor lassie! She had dared all to reclaim her stolen bauble – exactly what Lady Maisie herself would have done – and now she had to tramp home alone, save for her brave wee defender.

At last, reaching the Meadows, Rowan slowed down. If she kept running at full tilt she might attract attention. After all, a young girl carrying a dog out alone at night— What time was it, anyway? Mum must be frantic with worry, phoning around her friends, sending Robert out to search the streets. Rowan glanced at her watch and saw, to her amazement, that it was barely nine o'clock. If Will had left their house at eight, it meant that the seemingly endless adventure had actually taken place in under an hour. Rowan had the sensation of living in some alternative reality where time had no meaning and being pursued by a mysterious medallion-snatcher was an ordinary occurrence. And even if she told her family what had happened, how could they possible believe her?

However, when she finally turned in at her gate, it was to see the house looking exactly the same as usual. There was no light in the hall, no sign of a panic-stricken family combing the streets. Had she really not been missed?

'Don't they know I'm not there?' she whispered to Atholl.

The Scottie, who had been resting his front paws on her shoulder so that he could look backwards, on the alert for pursuit, licked her ear. She hugged his hot little body and then set him down on the grass. Atholl, his work done, trotted a little stiffly over the lawn and disappeared through a hole in the hedge.

Rowan felt extraordinarily cold without him as she crept into the hall. The television murmured from the sitting room, there was a line of light under the door of Robert's study, and from Bryony's room came the whine of one of her favourite singers.

Her family hadn't even noticed her absence! Rowan knew that she ought to be relieved to be escaping punishment for sneaking out after dark, but actually this seemed like the final straw. All the time that she had been in deadly danger Bryony and Mum – she didn't really count Robert – had been getting on with their boring old evening activities! Rowan's eyes filled with tears, and reaching her own wonderfully safe, warm room she flung herself face down on the bed, one hand holding Mr Bear's paw, and the other folded around the medallion.

Only then did Lady Maisie sink down into the rocking chair, tired and dispirited. She realized with a cold clutch of dread that her haunting days were almost over. This was no sorrow to her personally. She was old and weary, ready to rest beside her clan – but what if she faded away before she could save Rowan from whatever disaster Will McCantrip intended?

That would be no mere failure, but a mortal grief.

TEN

Rowan couldn't understand how she had slept at all after her terrifying adventure. Yet here she was, tucked up in her own bed, Mr Bear on guard, and the medallion still clutched in her hand.

'Rowan, wake up! We have to be at the dressmaker's for our fittings in half an hour!'

As Mum knocked on her door, Rowan instinctively slipped the chain over her head and tucked the medallion inside her nightie.

'And wear a skirt, please, not those ever-lasting jeans. We're going to Mollie's afterwards.'

All right growled Rowan to herself as she climbed out of bed. What did Mum care that she'd been chased through a deserted tenement by a mad American medallion-catcher?

Well, she didn't care because she didn't know – but Rowan couldn't tell her without giving away Alice's secret.

What she had to do was warn Bryony. Even she wouldn't be able to defend Will now. Rowan scrambled into her clothes and raced downstairs, only to find Robert alone in the kitchen.

'Where's Bryony? Is she still in her room?'

Robert put down his beloved boring newspaper. 'No, she's left already.'

'What?'

'She said she was going to the dressmaker's first and then she's meeting her friends Melanie and Sorcha to practise their music for the wedding.'

Melanie and Sorcha both played the fiddle.

'She's doing *what*?' repeated Rowan. 'She's actually going to play at the wedding? But she said she wouldn't!'

'I suspect she and the girls have been planning it all along,' Robert chuckled. 'And then, of course, once Will had offered to play, she didn't want to be left out.'

Rowan could hardly believe her ears.

'I daresay she wants to please her mother. Can I make you some toast?'

'Yeah, I suppose. I mean, thank you.' Rowan sank down at the table, watching Robert as he sliced and toasted the bread. She tried out one or two silent sentences. 'You'll never believe what happened last night!' Or 'You know, I don't think Will's really a student because—' No, she couldn't do it. Robert would never believe her, or if he *did* believe her, he'd want to call the police and she'd have to show them where Will lived – but she'd never find it again! The terrifying stair might be in any one of the alleys which opened off the Cowgate.

If only Bryony hadn't gone stravaiging off like that! Where was her only sister the one time she needed her? She probably wanted to get the dressmaker by herself, without Mum's interference.

'Rowan, you are wearing a clean shirt?'

Rowan's hand flew to her throat as Petronella entered, already draped in her cloak. She had thought it would be safer to

127

wear the medallion under her clothes than to leave it in the empty house, but she'd forgotten about undressing at Chantal's. What on earth was she to do?

She changed the clutching into a bit of toast-crumb brushing.

''Course it's clean,' she said.

'Do come *along*, darling.'

She could, oh – then, through the window, she saw Atholl trot out of the shrubbery, sit down and stare mournfully at the house. If he'd been wearing a watch, he would've looked at it.

'Atholl!' she exclaimed. 'Mum, I must just run out and say hello to him. He can't count, you know, so he doesn't know it's Saturday and he's waiting for me. I'll only be a minute.' And without waiting for an answer, Rowan hurried outside, her great idea pulsing through her head.

Lady Maisie had arisen early and, wrapping herself in her plaid, she skimmed over the rooftops to Will's attic. Once again the young man was dressing to go out, but today his thoughtwaves were so jagged with anger and despair that the ghost rubbed her hands together in glee.

'Aye, McCantrip, robbed by a lassie and a dog! That has ruffled your fine feathers, has it not, my wee callant?'

Will tugged on his remaining clothes, cursing as laces knotted and zippers jammed. Then, burying his head in his mighty cap, he stamped down the stairs and out into the close. As he made his way back towards the Grassmarket, passers-by stepped away from him, so powerful were the unseen rings of misery around him.

Lady Maisie followed, delighted to see that he was limping.

'Wounded by a tiny hound!' she exulted.

Will again turned in at the coffeehouse, sat himself down at a machine, and sent his fingers galloping over the keys.

'Dear Sis,

You won't believe this, I actually had my mitts on the treasure, but the kid set her dog on me. There was no sign of the pooch at supper, so I guess it must've been locked up

somewhere. Huge brute. All I could do was drop the locket and run. I was lucky to get away with my life. Perhaps you're right and I should've tried explaining things to Monteith, but he strikes me as pretty uptight.

But don't you give up hope, because I sure haven't.

Just wait until the next Gathering and we'll see who's leading the Clan McCantrip!

love,
Will'

Before the young man had time to despatch the message, there was a trilling in his pocket, and he whipped out one of the wee talking devices with which people now festooned themselves.

'Yeah?' he barked into it. 'Oh, er, yeah.'

To Lady Maisie's surprise, he was turning a dainty shade of pink and, hovering closer, she could just hear a tiny voice coming from the object. So mortals could now send spoken as well as written words through the crowded air?

'Um, sure, that would be cool. No,

nothing's wrong, it was just – OK, later, bye.'
Will put away the device, a bemused smile on
his hot face. Then he returned to his letter.

> **'P.S. Things are looking up
> already! New developments. That ol'
> McCantrip charm never fails.**
> **W'**

There was still no sign of Bryony when they
came home after lunch at Mollie's, so Rowan
phoned her friend, Lucy, who had a German
shepherd, collected Atholl and set out for a
good long walk along the banks of a nearby
stream. It gave her a nice safe feeling to be out
with a German shepherd because, as long as
she knew where the medallion was and Will
didn't, she felt she was in danger.

After the walk, she dropped off Atholl and
then went home by the street rather than
through the rustly back garden.

'Good heavens, Rowan, take your shoes off,
they're covered in mud. And I hope you didn't
let Atholl get dirty, you know how that upsets
Miss McFadzean.' Petronella was sitting at
the table, surrounded by wedding lists.

'So where's Bryony? Isn't she back yet?'

'No, she phoned to say she's going to some party with Melanie. She's taking Will with her.'

'She's doing *what*?' For the second time that day, Rowan sank into a chair.

'Will was saying the other night that he didn't know anyone in Edinburgh, so Bryony called him and asked him to come along.'

Rowan suddenly understood how parents must feel when their children begin going out at night.

'But where is this party? Who else is going?' How could Bryony bear to go anywhere with manky Will McCantrip? And she didn't know that he was not just manky, but plain dangerous!

'Rowan, please be quieter. You're shaking your head and stamping like a pony. I'm checking the replies to the invitations, I've got to have a bit of peace.'

'All right then, I'll go upstairs.'

Realizing that, until the wedding was over, she'd get even less sense out of her mother than usual, Rowan went to her room. Honestly, she and Bryony could both be wandering the dark streets pursued by berserk bagpipers and Mum wouldn't even notice!

ELEVEN

'Wake up, Bryony, I've got to talk to you!' Rowan advanced cautiously into her sister's bedroom. She'd actually lain awake until she'd heard Bryony come safely home the previous night and now she felt tired and cross, just like a parent.

'Rowan? Go away.' Bryony snuggled even deeper under her dark purple duvet. Sunday morning was never a good time to approach her.

'It's eleven o'clock. I've brought you some coffee. That special morning stuff you like.'

There being no room for the tray on the

bedside table, Rowan placed it on the floor. Then she raised the lid of the cafetière so that the delicious smell would drift in Bryony's direction.

Sure enough, Bryony pushed back her black mop of hair and sat up, nose twitching.

'You must really want something if you've made me coffee. Go on, pour me a cup then.'

Rowan opened the curtains and poured the coffee whilst Bryony put on her glasses and selected a radio station.

'So why are you sucking up to me like this? What's the big deal?'

'It's Will.' Rowan sat down on the bed. 'How on earth could you go out with him?'

'What business is it of yours what I do? And I didn't "go out with him". I took him over to Mel's so's he could meet that nerdy folk-singing sister of hers.'

'But Bryony, he's dangerous!'

'Dangerous?' Bryony, fired up with coffee and astonishment, was suddenly properly awake. 'Dangerous like a stale biscuit? You need your head examined.'

'No, I do not – and it's true. On Friday

night he stole the medallion but Atholl and I got it back!'

'That's not funny!'

'It's true!'

The sisters glared at one another, Bryony with her hair on end like a hedgehog awoken from hibernation, and Rowan equally angry and ruffled in her dressing-gown and slippers.

'Just wait till I tell you the whole story and then say it's not true.' And Rowan launched into the tale, from the medallion's loss to her safe return.

Bryony listened to the end, then reached for the cafetière and poured herself another cup. 'Actually, he was a bit odd last night. He kept asking if you'd said anything to me – and he wanted to know where we kept our dog! But when he realized I thought he was havering, he shut up.'

'What did I tell you?'

'But why would he want the medallion? And how did he know we had it?'

'You remember that first day I came home and found him here? He knew my name. He knows all about us!'

Despite the central heating, Rowan

shivered. Lady Maisie had awoken and drifted into the room.

So the sisters were holding a council of war, were they?

'I don't think that Will necessarily wants the medallion for a *bad* reason,' said Bryony. 'You're just assuming that. I mean, he's quite an OK person when you get past the scruffiness.'

'But Bry, he's totally manky and minging and horrible! His fingernails are all dirty and he always wears that naff hat!'

'You are so prejudiced. He knows a lot about music and he doesn't play half badly.'

'Just because he can play the boring old bagpipes doesn't cancel out the fact that he stole Alice's present.'

'But we don't know where she got it from, do we?'

'Wherever it came from, she meant Mum to have it.'

'There's only one way to find out.' Bryony balanced her coffee cup on a pile of books. 'We'll ask Will why he took it, and if he hasn't got a good reason, we'll have to tell Robert.'

'I'm not going back to that squat of

his!' The very idea make Rowan shudder.

'I'm meeting him this afternoon at the Museum of Scotland. We'll ask him then.'

'You arranged to meet him?' Rowan would no sooner have arranged to meet a rattlesnake.

'So what?' Bryony pushed back her duvet. 'He's very interested in his Scottish heritage, so I said I'd show him the museum. We're meeting at two o'clock. You come too and we'll ask him straight out.'

Valiantly said, lassie! declared Lady Maisie. She was as eager as the girls to learn why this once-noble clansmen had stooped to thievery.

Rowan got to her feet. 'Fine. But I can tell you that he'll need to have a pretty good excuse to make me forget how he chased me down all those stairs.'

And she flounced out of the room, Lady Maisie at her heels.

Lady Maisie had frequently visited the museum on her hauntings. It amused her to see perfectly ordinary objects – porridge bowls and spoons and such like – displayed in glass cases whilst the relics of her beloved Bonnie

Prince Charlie never failed to bring a tear to her eye.

On this occasion, however, the lassies had turned into the main hall, a chamber larger and higher than even the great banqueting hall of Clachanfeckle.

'Look, he's there already!' Rowan gripped Bryony's arm.

On a bench in the centre of the hall sat Will McCantrip. He was wearing his ridiculous hat but his beard had been trimmed and his plaid shirt had the rumpled look of a garment which had been washed but not ironed. Observing him amongst the well-dressed families with their cute little kids who were strolling between cafe and shop, Rowan felt less frightened of him. Then he glanced up and, seeing her with Bryony, he was the one to look alarmed.

'Bryony, hi,' he said, getting to his feet. 'Glad you could make it. And, er, you too, Rowan.'

As he said Rowan's name, he looked distinctly hangdog and shifty.

'Will,' said Bryony, 'we have to talk to you.'

Rowan had the impression that Will would very much like to make a run for it and she moved sideways, ready to cut him off. Not that she blamed him. Bryony, her hair twisted up into a dozen little spikes, nose-ring glinting, was a terrifying sight.

Will caught Rowan's movement and sank back down onto the bench, shoulders slumped, sneakered feet pushed out in front of him.

'Yeah,' he said. 'I reckon you do. Don't you guys have some saying like, "It's a fair cop"?'

'Yes, we do,' said Rowan, 'and that's what we want to know. Is it a fair cop? Why did you take our medallion?'

'No way is it *your* medallion!' Will straightened up. 'It belongs rightfully to *my* family, the McCantrips of Monteith.'

'What did I tell you!' exclaimed Bryony. She sat down beside Will. 'Go on, tell us the rest.'

Aye, go on, laddie, tell us! Tell us! demanded Lady Maisie. She had found it impossible to read his foreign, greedy thoughtwaves, crammed as they were with a longing for hot fried food.

'My ancestor, the one who sailed to Virginia, was a younger son of the Earl of Monteith, and when the family died out in

Scotland *we* should've become the earls.' Will sat up even straighter.

'So why didn't you then?' Interested despite herself, Rowan sat down on the bench.

'This was after the American War of Independence and my family had become real republicans. They didn't want anything to do with being lords and ladies.'

'But you've changed your mind about that, right?' said Rowan.

'No, I don't exactly want to be an earl. I just want to prove that I *could* be one if I wanted to, and to prove that I need the locket, medallion, whatever.'

Why? Why? raged Lady Maisie. Luckily for her impatient nature, Will carried on with his story.

'That locket was given to our ancestor's father by your King Charles II, and if I had it back it would prove that I'm the McCantrip of Monteith and I'd carry the fiery torch and Marie-Rose and I would lead all the other McCantrips at the Gathering!'

'What Gathering?'

'Who's Marie-Rose?'

Rowan and Bryony looked as blank as Lady Maisie felt.

'The Virginia Highland Gathering and Marie-Rose is my sister. She's—' Will paused for a moment and blinked '– she's a wheelchair-user. It would just mean so much to her to lead our clan.'

Rowan didn't quite know what to say. 'So what's stopping you from leading them right now?'

'This wealthy guy, Alvin McCantrip, the Used-Auto king. He got this family tree drawn up, showing that his kin have been in Virginia just about for ever, so he makes out he's the chieftain. But he sure ain't nobility like Marie-Rose and me!' Will sat up even taller, his furry hat looking almost like the proud bonnet of a clansman rather than a bit of acrylic fleece.

'I knew there was a good reason!' Bryony clasped her hands, for a terrible moment resembling Petronella.

'But if the medallion is so important to your family, how come you lost it?' said Rowan swiftly.

Will sighed. 'Typical family stuff. My grandfather was a quarrelsome old cuss, fought with everybody, and then emigrated as far west as he possibly could. When his wife died, my father – their only kid – quarrelled with the old man and came back to Virginia. The thing was, Grandfather still had the locket. My dad died a few years back, but before he passed over he told me about the locket and how it would prove our place in the clan. So when I decided that Marie-Rose was darn well going to lead the McCantrips, no matter how much money Alvin poured into that phoney family tree of his, I set off for Alaska.'

'Alaska!' exclaimed Rowan.

'Yes,' said Will. 'It took all my savings but I knew the old man was still alive and I hoped to find him and make up the quarrel but—' He paused dramatically '– I was too late! He died just a few days before I got there and the neighbour who'd been nursing him told me he'd given his one family heirloom to a young Scottish woman, a Mrs Monteith, who'd been passing through the town. He'd said that as his own family had never come near him, he wanted her to have it as he was related to the Monteiths.'

'So your grandfather gave the medallion to Alice?' said Bryony.

'And Alice must have wanted Mum to have it when *she* became the real Mrs Monteith. That must be why Alice told me to give it to Mum on her wedding day. But how did you know Alice had sent it to me?' said Rowan, still suspicious.

'Because Alice parcelled it up and asked the neighbour to give it to the bush pilot and the old lady remembered your name – Rowan Durwood – a tree and a wood, see, and that you lived in Edinburgh. So it was easy to find you, although at first I thought it was your mum who had been in Alaska and not the first Mrs Monteith. That sure confused me.'

Will was now looking rather pleased with himself.

'So you just walked into our house and set about stealing the medallion?' said Rowan sharply.

'Look, it wasn't like that. That first time, when you came home and found me, the door was wide open.'

The girls exchanged glances. Just what mum would do, especially in her excitement over the wedding.

Will caught their looks, and hurried on. 'I'd just come to check out your family, see if you looked like reasonable folks who'd believe me – and there was the front door, standing open.'

'So you came sniffing inside?' said Rowan.

Will had the grace to look ashamed. 'It was like it was *meant*, you know. An invitation. But I'd barely got in when you came home and I just panicked and said whatever came into my head, so I had to follow it up by pretending to be a student. Then I went to the reading to see the rest of your family and your mom was just so *nice* to me, inviting me round and asking me to play at the wedding and all – and I just didn't know how to ask for the locket back. I didn't even know if you had it.'

'That didn't stop you searching my room.' Rowan was determined not to be moved by Will's embarrassment. He was tugging at his earflaps as though he'd like to disappear inside his cap.

'I didn't exactly search your room,' he groaned. 'I just put my head round the door and it was lying there, almost begging me to take it home.'

Now it was Rowan's turn to look uncomfortable. She hadn't told Bryony how very careless she had been.

'So I grabbed it and vamoosed. I know I should've gone through the whole story with your parents, but it just seemed so much easier that way – until you came after me with that guard dog of yours. How come I didn't see him at supper? Was he tied up or something?'

Rowan might've laughed at this description of Atholl if she hadn't been so angry. 'No matter how you dress it up, you stole the medallion and then chased me down these stairs!'

'And your dog took a chunk out of my ankle! I should be suing you for assault!'

'And we should be charging you with theft!'

'Keep your voices down or we'll get thrown out,' said Bryony commandingly.

Rowan and Will sank back into their places whilst Lady Maisie, who loved a good brawl, quivered with disappointment.

'The thing is,' continued Bryony, '*we* say the medallion's ours, because Alice gave it to us, and *you* say it's yours because it's been in your family for yonks. So who's right?'

'I am,' said Will promptly.

Both girls looked at him.

'Just let me see it and I'll prove it to you. It opens up—'

'It opens?' exclaimed Rowan.

'Yeah, it's a locket, so it opens up, right, and engraved inside there's the letters CR with a crown, that's your King Charles, *Carolus Rex* in Latin, on one side, and on the other, the McCantrip clan crest, a mastiff rampant with a thistle between its teeth.'

A dog seemed a pretty inappropriate crest for Will, who'd just been bitten, but to Rowan it seemed safer not to mention this. Instead she said, 'I never thought of trying to open it.'

'So that's where you were wrong, see, and I'm right. How could I possibly know about the inscription if my dad hadn't told me?'

For a long moment, neither girl spoke. Then Bryony got to her feet. 'C'mon, we'll get this sorted out one way or the other.'

Will jumped up eagerly, but Rowan rose more slowly. She couldn't bear to think that all she and Atholl had gone through on Friday night was for nothing.

'It'll be such a pity if Mum can't wear it at her wedding,' she mourned.

'What's that?' Will, heading briskly for the exit, stopped in his tracks.

'Alice wanted us to give it to Mum on her wedding day,' explained Bryony.

'Aw, rats, I didn't know that. Like I said, you're mom's been so nice to me – but it's not for myself I want it, you know, it's for Marie-Rose. Look.' He pulled out his wallet and produced one of the photos which Rowan had pushed back so hurriedly. 'There's Marie-Rose.'

Lady Maisie curled herself around the girls' shoulders like a wisp of cold smoke in order to see the picture. It was the very one that the girls had already seen, Marie-Rose sitting stiff and cross in her wheelchair.

'Hates having her photo took,' said Will proudly.

Neither girl knew what to say.

'So, mmm, what happened?' said Bryony eventually.

'School bus ran into Mavis Creek.'

Rowan felt, simultaneously, cross and sniffly. Poor Marie-Rose was so much less pretty than Mum. The locket would simply look clumsy round her frail neck, but she needed it all the more for that very reason. 'I suppose it would be a very big deal for her to lead your clan?' she said.

'I'll say.' Will tucked the photo lovingly back into his wallet. 'And it would be a big boost for wheelchair-users everywhere. She'd even get on TV.'

'Terrific,' said Rowan faintly.

Lady Maisie was equally downhearted. She had never seen a wheelchair before and could not understand why the lassies had been so horribly impressed by it. What she did understand was that all the fight had gone out of Rowan. She was hirpling along, as dismal as a wet sark. And the ghost shared her feelings. All that haunting for nothing!

Will and Bryony, however, swung along in fine fettle. Discovering that they both liked the same especially miserable singer, Bryony had become almost animated whilst Will, despite the rain which was again falling, took off his cap and waved it in agreement. Rowan, trailing along behind them, realized that he must actually have washed his hair. His ponytail looked almost jaunty.

As they turned into Dryburgh Place, Rowan was surprised to see Robert drive past them.

'Who was that in the car with Robert?' she exclaimed. 'It looked like Miss McFadzean.'

'Was that Robert? I didn't notice,' said Bryony.

If it was Miss McFadzean, where was Atholl? Rowan hurried into the house.

'Mum, was that Robert and Miss McFadzean we saw in the car just now?' she called.

Petronella was on her way upstairs, a dainty tray of herb tea and biscuits in her hands. Seeing Rowan, she put the tray down on the hall table.

'Rowan, darling, do try not to be too upset, but there's bad news. Atholl's missing.'

'Missing!' Rowan's heart gave one huge painful thud.

'Yes, Miss McFadzean came round in the most frightful tizz. Apparently he stayed out all night – that didn't worry her at first – but when he didn't come back for breakfast or lunch—'

'We've got to look for him!' Rowan turned desperately to Bryony and Will.

'Miss McFadzean's already searched all around here and Robert's taking her to the police station now with a description and a photo. Then he's going to run up some Lost Dog posters on his computer, so we're already doing all we can.'

'We can split up and look again. We've got to find him!' Rowan felt that if she didn't take some action straight away her nerves would come sizzling right out of her skin.

'Do calm down, darling, pets get lost and found again all the time.' Petronella picked up her tray. 'Now I simply must have my afternoon nap. I'd bet you anything you like that by the time I wake up he'll have come trotting home again.' And giving the brave, sweet smile with which she had once bewitched audiences, Petronella disappeared upstairs.

'Right, let's start looking.' Rowan headed for the door.

'Hold on,' said Bryony, 'I know you're upset that Atholl's gone walkies, but if he's been gone since last night, surely we can sit down and have a cup of coffee first and make a plan of action?'

'Who is this Atholl?' said Will suspiciously. 'He's not the dog who—'

'That doesn't matter now!' Rowan almost screamed. 'We've got to find him!'

'But wait, he's got an identity tag, hasn't he?' said Bryony. 'Someone'll find him and turn him in.'

'No, no,' moaned Rowan, burying her face in her cold hands. 'You don't understand. He wasn't wearing his tag. I'd swapped it for the medallion!'

TWELVE

'You *what*?' Bryony's face, already powdered white, could not go any paler, but Will turned the colour of sour cream.

'You did *what*?' he squeaked.

'It seemed such a good idea at the time,' Rowan wailed. One small tear trickled down her cheek but she brushed it away. She *would not* cry in front of the teenagers. 'I couldn't hide it in my room again—' She looked meaningfully at Will. '– and I couldn't wear it myself because I'd have to take my things off at the dressmaker's, and then I saw Atholl through the window and it just came to me –

so I ran outside and changed the tag for the medallion. I knew Miss McFadzean was too shortsighted to notice and it was the one place Will wouldn't look.'

Will's face went from white to red.

'But *Rowan*—' Bryony, after one look at Rowan's expression, said no more. Instead, she hustled Rowan and Will into the kitchen and shut the door. 'OK. So now we *have* to have coffee, tea, whatever.' Will opened his mouth to protest, but she shoved him into a chair. 'It's *done*. There's no point in rabbiting on about it. We've got to decide what to do.'

Whilst Bryony put the kettle on, Rowan dug out some comforting biscuits, wondering if Bryony's practical streak came from their forgotten father. It certainly wasn't from Mum.

'Right,' said Bryony, slamming the mugs down onto the table. Such was the urgency of the occasion that she had made instant rather than ground coffee. 'What we need is a plan of campaign.'

Lady Maisie, who was flying in furious circles overhead, agreed totally. If anyone could have seen her, face flushed and light of battle in her eyes, they would have understood why her clansmen had been prepared to follow her to the death.

'Aye, lassies! To the rescue! The valiant hound must be snatched from whatever doom has befallen him.'

And without waiting to hear Bryony's words, she swooped through the window and out over the darkening city.

'Heaven's sakes, darlings, what long faces! I can't have you looking like that tomorrow. I want happy bridesmaids.'

It was Tuesday evening, and Petronella had entered the kitchen laden with gift-wrapped packages.

Rowan slouched down further into her chair. 'We've been putting up more of Robert's Lost Dog posters,' she said.

'So the poor little thing hasn't turned up yet?'

'If he had, we'd hardly be slogging round the streets putting up posters,' said Bryony.

'You needn't be sarcastic.' Petronella put the packages on the table. 'Wedding pressies. I told people we weren't expecting anything. After all, it's not as though Robert and I were

a young couple, but they've been pouring in!'
She took off her cloak, still chattering. 'And
it's been such a beautiful afternoon now that
the rain's finally stopped. I've just come from
Mollie's and the garden looks wonderful. If
the weather holds up we can have the ceremony out of doors.' The smallest flicker of
worry crossed her face. 'I want everything to
be perfect.'

Rowan, Bryony, and Lady Maisie, who was
stretched out along the top of the dresser, all
sighed.

'Now, girls, I'm just as upset as you are
about Atholl but we mustn't let it spoil the big
day.'

Your big day, thought Rowan savagely.
You don't care a hoot what happens to Atholl.
Then she forced herself to calm down. After
all, Mum didn't know the whole terrible story.
Oh *why* had she swapped Atholl's tag?
What if someone had spotted the medallion
and kidnapped him? What if he'd fought to
defend it and—? These terrible ideas had
been trampling round and round in her head
until she felt like howling. No wonder she
looked miserable.

She put on a brave face for Mum's benefit.

'Of course we won't look gloomy tomorrow but I'll nip out after supper and have another look for Atholl. Just in case.'

'Certainly not! You were out searching all Sunday evening and after school yesterday but tonight you simply must wash your hair. The hairdresser's going to put it up for you when he comes to do mine in the morning. You too, Bryony.'

'But—'

'And early to bed. Now, Robert's not coming back to cook, he's at Mollie's making some roulade thing for the veggies, so I thought, for a treat, we'd order in pizzas.'

They'd always had pizza on special occasions when they'd lived in Yarrow Row, but Robert despised take-outs. For a moment, Rowan saw such a clear picture in her head of their old kitchen, Bryony and herself watching *Neighbours* and eating chips with their fingers whilst Mum prepared her lessons for the next day, all the things which they didn't do in Robert's house, that she very nearly burst into tears.

'Yeah,' said Bryony quietly. 'Pizza would be good.'

*   *   *

Lady Maisie awoke with a jolt. She had fallen asleep, totally exhausted. Time after time, for the past two days, she had tracked the woolly thoughtwaves of some ambling pet only to find a common cur or disdainful poodle. She had asked every ghoul and poltergeist on her path to be on the look-out. She had roamed from the templed top of Calton Hill to the depths of Leith Docks.

But she had failed to find Rowan's doggy companion and a McNeil never failed!

Now, awoken by a strange spicy smell, she propped herself upon on one elbow and looked down on the room. The lassies were tearing at some foreign foodstuff with their fingers – not the sort of behaviour which they employed in Monteith's presence – and something about Rowan's posture awoke a distant memory in the ghost. The child was thinking so hard about the lost hound that Lady Maisie could almost see him, crouched by the lassie's plate. Where, in all her hauntings, had she seen a child sharing a rough meal with a Scottie dog, snatching the crusts with thin hands before scurrying off amongst the gravestones? Then the memory clicked into place. How could she have been such a foolish wraith? In all of old

Edinburgh was there not one certain place where a lost dog would seek refuge?

Lady Maisie shook out her skirts and straightened the jewelled combs in her hair. One must look one's best for a visit to a kirkyard.

THIRTEEN

It was sad that she couldn't enjoy being beautiful.

Rowan looked at herself in Mollie's spare room mirror and sighed. She wasn't usually even pretty, but today,with her hair done up in an elegant knot and wearing her long silk dress with discreet tartan trim she looked completely different. Like an elf. Or an illustration out of her old *Flower Fairy* books. But she just couldn't appreciate it because all she could think about was Atholl.

She had rushed over to Miss McFadzean's before breakfast to discover that Atholl still hadn't come home and that his mistress was beside herself with worry. Rowan simply hadn't known whether or not to explain about the missing name-tag, but then Robert had called her and she'd fled guiltily home.

Then after breakfast – a cup of tea in Rowan's case, black coffee for Robert and Bryony, and herb tea and toast and honey for Petronella, 'I simply must keep my strength up' – Robert had driven the family over to Mollie's. Robert had been white with tension and Mum totally hyper which was peculiar, Rowan thought, given that they'd both been married before. Perhaps getting married was always nerve-shattering, no matter how often you did it.

Mollie's house, when they arrived there, was already buzzing with excitement. All of Mollie's family plus several of Petronella's friends were running around with plates of food and bowls of flowers. Dozens of small children were being swatted out of the way by the helpers and some elderly guests were sitting on the sunny terrace with a bottle of wine. Everyone was busy and happy.

Everyone except Rowan and Bryony.

And now Rowan stood in front of the mirror in her useless splendour whilst behind her Bryony wriggled into her dress.

'Mirror hog,' said Bryony.

'Sorry.' Rowan slouched over to the window. It was the beautiful day which Mum had longed for and Mollie's garden, which lay in a curve of the river, was a sunlit patch of lawns and roses. As she watched, some of the older children began to carry out chairs and arrange them on the grass. Will must be around somewhere, grieving over the lost medallion and his sister's disappointment.

'Zip me up.'

Rowan did as she was told, and then stepped back.

Bryony's black dress with tartan-ribbon straps was tighter than hers, with a long slit up one side. Obviously Mum had not realized that Bryony was going to wear sheer black stockings with lacy tops under it.

'Has Mum actually *seen* your dress? When you sit down to play the clarsach, won't everyone see your stocking tops?'

'So?'

'And what's that on your arm?' Rowan stared with a mixture of awe and horror at the swirly Celtic design. 'It is just henna, isn't it?'

Bryony licked her finger and ran it over the tattoo. 'What do you think?'

'Bry! Mum'll go spare!'

'All she said was, lose the nose-ring.'

Sure enough, Bryony's nose was unadorned.

'But when did you get it done?'

'Two weeks ago. Straight after the dress-maker's.'

'Oh *Bryony*.'

'Oh Bryony so what? At least I *know* when I'm doing something mental.'

'It was not mental. Hiding the medallion was a dead good idea. At the time.'

There was a knock at the door, and both girls spun round.

'Can I come in? It's Will.'

Rowan caught her breath. Will, like them-selves, had been searching the streets, but in a frenzy which she found slightly scary.

'Come in, we're decent,' called Bryony.

The door opened slowly to reveal Will in a full dress kilt, doublet with ruffles, knee socks, laced brogues and a splendid silver-mounted sporran.

Rowan so very nearly began giggling out of sheer nervousness that she had to dig her nails into the palms of her hands. Poor Will was a pitiful sight. The borrowed kilt was too short, showing his skinny knees, whilst the black doublet made his skin look even pinker and more freckled than usual.

'No news?' he said huskily. Then he stopped and stared at Bryony. 'Great dress,' he said. 'I was expecting something more, like, traditional, but that's cool.'

'I don't do tradition,' said Bryony, 'and there's no news. Not a whisker.'

'How am I gonna tell Marie-Rose? This is just gonna break her heart.' Will paced over to the window, and stared out, as Rowan had done. 'She would love it here. Puts me in mind of Mavis Creek, with the river and all. Although it sure is high.'

'It's in spate,' said Rowan dully. 'All that rain.'

'Marie-Rose used to like nothing better than taking the old boat out, but now she can't swim any more, we've gotta be real careful. We only go out when the water's low.'

Every one of Will's words added to the weight on Rowan's heart. Not only had she put Atholl in danger but she had also destroyed the crippled girl's dream of leading her clan.

'I'm going downstairs,' she said. 'Shouldn't you be playing by now, Bryony?'

'Probably. I'll be down in a minute.'

Rowan walked as steadily as possible down the curved staircase and into the large room whose French windows gave on to the garden. People were already gathering on the lawn and, as she passed, relatives and friends greeted her. Rowan smiled politely and slipped through the crowd, feeling oddly like a ghost. It didn't seem as though she were really there, in her pretty dress, when the most important part of herself was crying, Oh Atholl, where are you?

And then, through the happy murmur of the crowd, she heard something wonderfully familiar. A crisp, commanding bark.

'Atholl!'

Rowan picked up her long skirt and raced across the grass towards the white Scottie who was bounding straight for her, his lovely paws barely touching the ground. She was about to fling herself down beside him but Miss McFadzean, who was scurrying along in his wake, cried: 'Your dress, dearie, your dress!' And indeed, Atholl himself seemed to realize the importance of keeping Rowan's dress clean as instead of leaping up on her he simply sat down, wagging his tail ferociously.

Rowan, speechless, bent down to caress him.

'He came trotting in the front gate, nice as ninepence, and just in time for me to get him dressed up for the wedding. But the oddest thing, I was tying to bow to his collar and I noticed—'

'There he is! He's got it, he's got the McCantrip treasure!'

Miss McFadzean turned and blinked, her large straw hat quivering. Several other people also turned towards the wild figure who was running across the lawn, sending infants flying and old people tottering out of his way.

Rowan straightened up as Will advanced. 'Calm down, Will,' she said, 'I'll get it for you.'

Lady Maisie, who had flung herself down upon a delightfully soft, grassy bank, wearily got back to her feet as Will, ignoring Rowan, made straight for the little dog.

Surely there had been enough havers for one day, exclaimed the tired ghost. She had found the Scottie as she'd suspected, sleeping beneath a bush in Greyfriars' Kirkyard, the very place where, all those years before, the faithful Greyfriars' Bobby had kept watch beside his master's grave. Where else would a little dog go but to the spot where the famous terrier had spent his last years, fed by the keeper of the neighbouring tavern?

If finding Atholl had been easy, leading him home had been a different matter. *Rowan gave me this new tag. She said I had to keep it safe. This is the safest place I know*, ran his stubborn, doggy thoughtwaves. He knew that Lady Maisie was there but he snapped at her commands and kept running in the opposite direction. It had taken all Lady Maisie's will-power, plus the aid of a kindly passing vampire, to drive him back to his own garden.

Now she felt that she could not float another inch – yet it looked as though her help was about to be needed yet again.

Will, catching the tell-tale glint of gold at Atholl's collar, pounced, but Atholl bared his teeth in an eager snarl. Rowan had entrusted the token to him and he would never give it up.

'Wait, Will, I'll get it from him!' shrieked Rowan but Will, maddened by the sight of his lost heirloom, elbowed her out of the way and seized Atholl's collar.

Atholl dug his teeth into Will's wrist, wriggled free and took off between the startled guests.

Will, swearing horribly and clutching his wrist, ran after Atholl, blood raining down upon his borrowed kilt whilst Rowan and Bryony raced in pursuit. Guests fell back on either side of the chase, all very unclear as to what was happening. Was this some ancient Celtic wedding ritual?

Will, with his long legs and unencumbered by a posh dress, was catching up on Atholl. The Scottie dog, his wee legs going like clockwork, ran between the trees which marked the edge of the garden and found himself on the brink of the river. The water surged past, striking the curves of the bank and spinning out into a dozen crosscurrents. The little dog didn't hesitate. As Will's outstretched hand touched his fluffy tail, Atholl flung himself into the torrent.

And without a thought for his own safety, Will leapt in after him.

'Atholl!'

'Will!'

The two girls stood screaming on the bank as first the dog and then the young man were swept from sight.

Lady Maisie, hovering above them, plaid unloosed and curls streaming down her white shoulders, summoned up every last molecule of ghostly power. Perhaps she would never again see the lovely banks of Loch Rannoch, never again haunt the wynds of old Edinburgh. Perhaps this leap would be her last.

But no matter! The honour of the McNeils was at stake!

With one eldrich cry, so piercing that Rowan and Bryony heard it and thought it an echo of their own, Lady Maisie threw herself into the surging foam.

For a split second she was actually visible, the lace edge of her petticoat blending with the ripples, her long hair tossed out into the rushing brown water. Rowan almost glimpsed this third figure disappearing into the river but all her thoughts were on Atholl.

how could he possibly survive the torrent?

She ran along the bank, stumbling in her silly smart shoes, Bryony close behind her. At this point, the river tumbled over a weir and then curved out of sight beyond a bed of flooded rushes. The two girls panted over the soggy ground, scarcely believing that they would ever see boy or dog again, and only dimly aware of the uproar in the garden behind them.

Rowan pushed her way through the belt of small trees which screened the far side of the rushes – and saw Will struggling out of the river, water streaming down his ponytail and beard, his ruffles ruined, kilt drenched, weeds lodged in his sporran – but clutched in his arms, a half-drowned, squirming Scottie.

'Oh Atholl! Are you all right?'

'Will, you saved Atholl!'

Rowan kicked off her shoes and paddled through the rushes, arms outstretched. 'Atholl, Atholl, you brave dog!'

Will spat out a mouthful of water. 'What d'ya mean, brave dog? *I* rescued him, didn't I?'

'Only because you wanted the medallion.'

'I still rescued him.' Will, up to his stocking tops in mud, tightened his grasp on Atholl who was wriggling and whining, his gaze fixed apologetically on Rowan.

'Give him to me and I'll undo the medallion for you.'

'How do I know I can trust you?' Will actually took one squelching step backwards towards the river and Lady Maisie, who was lying on the bank, flat as a length of ribbon, uttered a moan of exasperation. If the daft lad flung himself into the water again, it would be the end of him and the hound. The ghost certainly could not propel them to the bank a second time. She had swept Atholl into Will's arms, seized Will under the oxters, shoved him into the one current which would hit the bank and then, using his sporran as a rudder, guided the pair to safety. She had managed it once, but twice would be beyond her.

'Will, have you gone totally barking?' Bryony had waded into the rushes after Rowan. In her tight black dress she looked like some elegant swamp creature. 'Give Atholl back and come away from the river *at once*.'

Will took one look at her and came obediently forward, his feet making great sucking noises as he dragged them clear of the mud.

He was about to place Atholl in Rowan's out-stretched arms when there was yet another wild cry from the bank.

'No, no, Rowan, your *dress*!'

Will, dripping with river water, and Rowan and Bryony, up to their ankles in mud, all spun soggily around and stared at Petronella. Framed prettily by the autumnal trees, her hair piled into an elaborate tower of ringlets, she stood above them, carefully holding up the skirt of the famous tartan wedding dress.

'Whatever are you doing? Your dresses, girls, your beautiful kilt, Will! Rowan, leave that wretched animal alone, he'll ruin your dress.'

Bryony was the first to find her voice. 'But Mum, Will saved Atholl's life. He jumped into the river and rescued him.'

'What was the silly animal doing in the river in the first place? Don't you realize that the registrar will be here any minute and she won't wait if we aren't ready!' There was a touch of hysteria in Petronella's voice.

'What are you girls playing at? Don't you realize the registrar—? Petronella!'

'Robert!'

Robert had come striding through the trees, but he stopped dead at the sight of Petronella in her tartan gown, white roses at her breast and jewelled clips in her hair. Petronella likewise, swirling round in a froth of petticoats, froze in admiration at the sight of her beloved. Robert was not showing his legs in a short, stitched modern kilt. No, his secrecy at an end, he stood before them in a splendid Braveheart outfit – loose white shirt, grey tweed sleeveless jerkin, and a kilt which was simply a length of plaid gathered round his waist like a sari with the end tossed over his shoulder. By his side swung a mighty claymore.

'Robert!' breathed Petronella. 'You look wonderful!'

'Petronella – Lady Maisie's dress! You must've been inspired!'

'I thought you would like it.' Petronella looked as modest as it was possible for a very pregnant woman to look. Rowan, climbing up the bank on cold wet feet thought of saying that it had been her idea, but decided against it. She'd already done enough to spoil Mum's wedding day.

'What on earth's been happening?' Robert put his hand on the hilt of his claymore rather as though he would slice through the main culprit.

Rowan, for the second time that day, managed not to burst into nervous giggles. 'Atholl jumped into the river and Will jumped in after him.'

'Atholl fell in and Will rescued him.' Bryony, carrying both pairs of shoes, climbed up after Will.

'Who cares any more?' said Rowan, worn out with emotion. 'At all events, Will rescued him so I suppose that makes him a hero.' She bent down to Atholl who was shaking himself vigorously and undid his collar. Then she slid the medallion onto her hand and thrust it at Will. 'There you go,' she said. 'One family heirloom.'

Will snatched the medallion, but then, as he ran his fingers over the tiny enamelled flowers, a look of reverence dawned on his wet pink face.

'At last! The McCantrip locket!'

'The what?' Robert asked.

'The registrar! My wedding!' Petronella exclaimed.

Robert and Petronella were looking completely bewildered.

'The heirloom which proves that I am clan chieftain. Look!' Will ran his nail down the side of the medallion and it opened like a little book.

'It is a locket!' exclaimed Rowan. 'I always thought it was solid.'

Will held it out and she saw, just as he had predicted, on one side, the curly, crowned letters CR, and on the other, a tiny dog grasping a thistle between his teeth.

'Let me see – where did you get that?' Robert, in his turn, grabbed the locket. 'Good grief – Charles II!'

'Robert – the *time*!' wailed Petronella.

'Pet, sweetie, the registrar's here!'

'Where's the wedding party?'

'Will – your kilt!'

Mollie, Mollie's husband and several more friends were arriving on the scene, each one adding some new cry of amazement or dismay. Those who appeared first explained things to later arrivals.

'The piper saved the wee dog's life.'

'Who is he anyway?'

'Some famous American champion.'

Will drew himself up to his full height. He shook the waterweed out of his hair and straightened his dripping ruffles. 'Petronella,' he said solemnly, 'this is the very locket which your good king Charles II gave to my ancestor, the McCantrip of Monteith, and I have to take it home to Marie-Rose so that she can wear it at the Virginia Gathering, but I'd be honoured if you'd wear it on your wedding day.'

'Why, Will!' Petronella looked at the beautiful golden locket as it rested on his grubby hand. 'The honour would be mine.'

She took one of the ribbons from her sleeve, threaded it through the locket's loop, and with Robert's help, tied it round her throat.

Yes, Rowan thought, she'd been right. It *was* the finishing touch and Lady Maisie, who had laboured up the bank, barely able to float, wholeheartedly agreed. Mistress Petronella might be a fool but she did indeed look bonnie on her wedding day.

Mollie, meanwhile, had seized Will by the arm and was rushing him towards the house to change into an old kilt of her husband's whilst the other guests returned to the lawn, spreading still wilder versions of the dramatic rescue.

Rowan and Bryony wiped their feet on

the grass, put on their shoes, and followed the bridal couple back into the garden. Atholl trotted after Rowan, head and tail high. He didn't quite understand everything which had happened, but he knew that he had done his duty.

'But why did Atholl have Will's heirloom?' Robert, although holding Petronella gallantly by the hand, was still torn by historical curiosity.

'Robert, we have to get married today! We have to get married *now*!'

'It's a long story,' said Rowan. 'Tell you later. Look, everyone's waiting.'

Sure enough, the wedding guests were assembled on the lawn, the women's hats nodding and bobbing as they asked one another the reason for the delay. Was it true that the world-famous musician had leapt into the river to rescue his pipes, which had been snatched by a gigantic mad dog? Then, as the bridal couple emerged from the trees, the two maids gliding demurely behind them, all heads turned and there was a collective sigh of delight. Robert looked so handsome in his kilted plaid! Petronella was so beautiful and what a unique dress! And her lovely daughters were absolute nymphs! And that adorable little Scottie dog!

The registrar, in her smart dark suit, stopped fidgeting and looking at her watch. Bryony's two friends, who had been fiddling valiantly through the kerfuffle, struck up *Amazing Graze*, the congregation joined in and Robert and Petronella advanced with dignity.

Lady Maisie found her eyes filling with tears. She knew the old tune well, and the sight of Mistress Petronella in her own favourite gown and Monteith looking the spit of her own brave clansmen touched her Scottish heart to the core. Never again would she see so brave a sight!

Rowan, standing behind Mum and Robert, also found herself tearful, but through sheer relief. Atholl was safe. Will would get his wretched locket back, and with any luck, he'd hightail it to Virginia and they'd never see his ginger head again. And Mum did look pretty and Robert had been cunning enough to cover up his knees, and she could enjoy wearing her lovely dress.

A tiny warm breeze sent a drift of red leaves over Mum and Robert, and one of Rowan's tears escaped onto her cheek. As she raised her hand to brush it away, she saw, from the corner of her eye, Bryony make the same gesture.

FOURTEEN

The wedding celebrations continued unchecked for several hours. Will, arrayed in an older, longer kilt and a plain shirt, piped outdoors. Bryony and her friends played more quietly inside. Toasts were drunk, Robert sliced the cake with his claymore, the delicious food was eaten, the small children grew over-excited on sips of champagne, Atholl ate half a grilled chicken and fell asleep, and the guests threw off their shoes and danced on the soft grass – the Dashing White Sergeant, the Eightsome Reel, and Marie's Wedding!

Lady Maisie, perched on a low tree, was sobbing so hard that the white rose on her breast brimmed with tears. This was surely the last time that she would see these dear old dances. And how nimbly Rowan spun down the set! She had never thought to care for a mortal but something about the child reminded Lady Maisie of her own youth. It was sad to think that she would not see her grow up but the ghost knew that her watery leap had taken the last of her strength.

'Farewell!' she mourned, as she drifted, one last time, down the length of the dance.

Rowan was spinning along the set, dizzy with champagne and sheer delight. At the foot, she and her partner crossed hands and birled, the other dancers, the musicians, the Japanese lanterns which hung in the trees, all melting into one another before her eyes.

'Rowan! Rowan!' Surely someone was calling her name?

Rowan slowed down, but before she could plunge back into the dance Bryony grabbed her hand and dragged her clear.

'Bryony, I can't stop now, it'll break up the set!'

'They'll have to improvise.' Bryony's gelled

hair was standing straight up in wild spikes. 'Listen, Mum's gone into labour, Robert's just taken her to the hospital!'

'She's done *what*? But isn't it early?'

'Only a few days – she thinks she got the dates wrong, you know Mum.'

'No wonder she was in such a hurry.'

'Robert says we've got to stay here tonight.'

'Not go to the hospital?'

'So he *says*.' Bryony looked meaningfully at Rowan and Rowan looked meaningfully back.

'We can get a taxi on the main road, can't we? Have you got any money?'

'In my jacket. Hold on a minute, Mum asked me to give this back to Will.' She opened her hand to reveal the locket.

Rowan looked at it for the last time, realizing that she simply didn't care any more what happened to it. 'OK,' she said.

Bryony darted off between the dancers, leaving Rowan hopping with impatience. Typical Mum, having her baby at her own wedding. If there was a dramatic way of doing something, she would find it.

Lady Maisie paused in her sorrowful circuit of the dance. So the mistress was on her childbed? Aye, that was the way of the world, as one soul returned to its resting place, another was born . . . the ghost quivered as her final, best idea flared up in her breast.

'C'mon, Bry,' Rowan muttered under her breath.

Bryony was talking earnestly to Will, who had stopped playing to listen to her. Now she was pressing the locket into his hand, and with a final word, she turned and hurried back towards Rowan.

'What took you so long?'

'Just arranging to meet Will again before he goes home.'

So perhaps Rowan hadn't seen the last of Will and his scrubby ginger ponytail? However she said, 'Don't let Mollie see us, let's just grab our jackets.'

Fortunately, few of the other guests were aware of the bride's dramatic departure, so the girls were able to slip out of the house unnoticed. Then it was only a short distance to the main road where they found a taxi almost at once.

'Thank goodness.' Rowan sank back onto the comfy seat. 'Can't we tell the driver it's a matter of life and death?'

'No, we can't,' said Bryony. 'It's not so far. We'll be there in fifteen minutes.'

'Perhaps she'll have had the baby by then.'

'No she won't.'

Lady Maisie, her wide skirts crammed into the small space, was equally impatient. The journey would've taken no time at all on horseback.

'We're almost there – there's the hospital.'

'But that's the wrong entrance!'

'No it isn't, drivers always know stuff like that.'

'I hope so.'

The sisters were bickering out of nerves and exhaustion.

'Here we are, ladies. Maternity Department.' The driver looked at them curiously as Bryony paid him and they both raced into the building, Rowan's dress fluttering and the slit in Bryony's skirt revealing her long legs with every stride. Then the automatic doors sucked open and they were engulfed by the hot, bright, antiseptic air.

Rowan felt very conspicuous as they approached the reception desk.

'Yes?' The woman behind the desk looked

at them wearily, her expression not matching the bright smile of the photo on her identity tag.

'Our mother came in a short time ago, Mrs Monteith. We'd like to know how she's getting on,' said Bryony.

Rowan was impressed by her sister's confidence, especially as the woman continued to regard them warily. Perhaps kids weren't supposed to wander in by themselves?

'If you wait in the waiting room,' she said, nodding towards it, and then delayed picking up the phone until the girls were obediently seated there.

'Do you think Robert will be angry we've come?' whispered Rowan.

'Who cares?'

Bryony was right. Who cared what Robert thought? He wasn't their father. He wasn't going to stop them getting in on the excitement of having a new brother or sister – yes, an actual new little person – entering their family. For the very first time, Rowan felt a thrill of excitement. This baby might grow up to be her special friend. She'd take it for walks in its buggy and play with it and later on she'd teach it really useful stuff like the right clothes to wear and how to avoid being bullied.

'What are you girls doing here? Didn't I tell you to stay at Mollie's?'

Robert had appeared before them, his luxuriant hair rumpled and looking, to Rowan's satisfaction, absolutely green. Obviously watching a baby being born was a lot more gory than jointing a chicken or filleting a fish.

'How's Mum?' said Bryony.

'Is the baby born yet?' said Rowan.

'Fine, fine, no, not yet,' said Robert, running a trembling hand through his hair. 'But it won't be long now, so you girls just take a cab straight back to Mollie's and I'll phone you the minute it's all over.'

'We're staying here,' announced Bryony firmly.

'But there's no point, you won't be able to see the baby.'

'Yes, we will,' said Rowan. 'Mum definitely said that the hospital had a child-friendly policy.'

'That means that young people are allowed

to visit,' explained Bryony politely and they both looked at Robert with the cold stares which they knew would swiftly reduce him to emotional rubble.

It only took a few seconds. Robert flung up his hands and dashed along the corridor, disappearing through a distant swing door.

Time passed. Bryony did a quiz in one of the old magazines on the waiting room table, and Rowan, too strung-out to sleep, too tired to be really worried, fell into an odd daze in which someone seemed to be crooning a lullaby in her ear.

> *'O can ye sew cushions*
> *An' can ye sew sheets*
> *An' can ye sing baalaloo*
> *When the bairn greets?*
>
> *I'd be loathe tae leave ye*
> *I'd be loathe tae go,*
> *Perhaps I'll bide we' ye*
> *For a lifetime or so.'*

She recognized the first verse, but surely the rest of the words were wrong? She roused herself. 'Bryony, you remember that song we used to sing in Primary, *Can ye sew cushions*—?' but before she could finish, Robert had come bounding back down the length of the corridor, completely transformed from his previous, pallid self. Grinning more broadly than Rowan had ever seen him do before, he swept up to the girls and actually hugged them.

'A little girl!' he exclaimed. 'You've got a little sister!'

Rowan felt a huge, matching grin spreading over her own face. A little sister! She hadn't realized until that very moment how much she'd wanted a sister rather than a brother. A boy would soon have got into computers and football and hanging out with his mates but a girl would always be there, a friend for the rest of her life.

'Can we see her?'

'Just for a moment, the nurse says. Your mother's got to rest.'

'Mum's all right, isn't she?' said Bryony.

'Oh absolutely splendid, in better shape than I am. But of course she's been through it all before, hasn't she? Not like me.' And burbling happily, Robert ushered them ahead of him down the corridor.

The passages and stairs seemed endless, miles of vinyl which squeaked under their feet and dozens of doors which swung gently shut behind them.

'Here we are.'

A final corridor, a final door and a nurse coming out saying, 'Not more than two minutes, mind', and Rowan found herself in another hot, bright room, but with Mum sitting up in bed against a mound of snowy pillows, a tiny swathed bundle in her arms. Mum was looking even more beautiful than ever. Her cheeks were pink, her eyes glowed, and her hair curled around her face in golden spirals.

But it was the baby at whom Rowan stared.

'Isn't she beautiful?' said Petronella.

'Oh *yes*,' breathed Rowan.

'She's OK,' admitted Bryony.

'We'll have to name her after the heroine of one of Robert's books. Maybe Kenna from *A Scots Bluebell* or—'

Mum's voice lilted on in the background

whilst Rowan, suddenly puzzled, gently stroked her new sister's cheek. How could a tiny baby somehow look *familiar*? Where had she seen those hazel eyes, already alight with mischief and charm, and those wisps of light brown, curly hair?

And what a strong smell of roses there was in the room, stronger yet more delicate than any talcum powder.

'—or there's Jeanie from *Barefoot in the Heather* or—'

The baby fastened her little warm hand around Rowan's finger and looked her straight in the eye.

'Call her Maisie,' Rowan heard herself say. 'After Lady Maisie McNeil, the *Lassie wi' the White Rose*.'

'Yes,' agreed Bryony, 'she'll grow up to be a really strong, independent woman if you call her after Lady Maisie.'

'What rubbish,' said Robert. 'How can a little baby grow up into a name?'

Three, no, four pairs of eyes looked commandingly at him.

'Oh very well then, if that's what you've all decided. Maisie it is.'

Rowan wriggled her finger within the baby's tight clasp.

'Hello, Maisie,' she whispered.

And Maisie smiled, the wise smile of a very much older person.

THE END

GHOST ON THE LOOSE
Helen Dunwoodie

*As she climbed towards the half-landing, Rowan
found herself mysteriously compelled to slow
down. What was so special about Robert's room
that he wouldn't allow anyone else inside it?*

For Rowan it is bad enough having to live with
Robert, Mum's boring new boyfriend, without
his ridiculous obsession with his study. What
can he be hiding there that is so important?
Or so horrible?

Rowan's not the only one who's intrigued by the
study. In fact, there's someone who's discovered
Robert's secret and is determined to expose him.
The only problem is that Lady Maisie McNeil is
a ghost and she can't wreak her revenge without
a bit of help from someone in the twentieth
century. It looks like she's found just the girl . . .

**'A stylish and funny tale for nine to
twelve-year-olds'**
The Times

**'A brilliantly written story about
step-families learning to get on,
mysteries and ghosts'**
Young Book Trust 100 Best Books of 1999

CORGI YEARLING BOOKS

SOLO ACT
Helen Dunwoodie

*Iris has the looks, the voice, the confidence
. . . so why is everything going wrong for her?*

First Jimmy Garcia, the new (and *very*
fanciable) director of her drama group, has
the nerve to criticize her acting. In front of
everyone! Then, when he announces his
plan to take their show to the world-famous
Edinburgh Fringe Festival, Iris's mother
starts being really difficult about her going.

Iris *knows* she's good enough to make it –
and knows that stardom doesn't come easy.
But why does it have to be *so* hard?

**'Dunwoodie sweeps the reader along in
a most agreeable and enjoyable way'**
Books for Keeps

**'An all-round excellent read for the
stage-struck and those looking for a
deeper account of human relationships'**
Carousel

For older readers

0 552 545244

CORGI BOOKS